THE KINCANNON LEGACY

LAST WILL
& TESTAMENT

BOOK ONE

Jordan L. James

Sharyn G. Jordan

The Kincannon Legacy – Last Will and Testament

eBook ISBN: 978-1-965761-25-0
Paperback: 978-1-965761-26-7
Ingram Spark ISBN: 978-1-965761-27-4
Library of Congress Control Number: 2025900873

Disclaimer: This book merges historical fiction and a political thriller. While it draws inspiration from actual events, people, and places, the narrative is a product of the Authors' imagination. Names, characters, and incidents have been altered or fictionalized to enhance the story and protect the identities of those involved. Certain characters may be composites of various historical figures, and creative liberties have been taken to dramatize the story. The authors have exercised artistic license in weaving together fact and fiction to create a compelling narrative. Readers are encouraged to approach this book as a blend of history and imagination rather than a factual account and to keep an open mind. The journey is indeed an adventure of the soul.

Publisher/Editor: Triangulus 3 Publishing, LLC
Images: Adobe Stock
Book Cover Design: Angie Alaya
Book Layout: Marigold2k

CONTENTS

Dedicated
to
Shawn Lewis Hathcock

White. A blank page or canvas.
So many possibilities.

~Stephen Sondheim

Acknowledgements

With profound gratitude,
Becky Bee Norwood
Bonnie Tyminski

*We maintain that thanks is the highest
form of thought and that gratitude
is happiness doubled by wonder.*

~G. K. Chesterton

PROLOGUE

Last Will & Testament

Finnegan "Finn" Padraig Kincannon

To Whom It May Concern:

Being of unsound mind, I declare this my *Last Will and Testament,* revoking any previous codicils I made.

Thank you to my cherished family and friends; you have been incredibly supportive of me throughout my life. You exemplify and have nurtured the values I hold dear. Reflecting on the power of community, a bright spirit shines through, dispelling any darkness.

As my quill glides smoothly across the parchment paper, each word is a glowing tribute to my inspiring intentions, expressing deep gratitude for the magical, miraculous, and loving life I have lived.

Honorably, I bequeath the following:

To my mother, Joy Elisabeth Kincannon, I leave my treasured collection of musical scores, manuscripts, and poetic works. May you find encouragement and solace in my creations. Thank you, Mom; you were always there for me and supported my compelling drive to improve the world.

To my paternal Grandmother, Grace Gayle "Gawni" Kincannon: I leave you with my journal, which contains my thoughts, hopes, and visions for a better future. I am returning the cherished books you gifted me. The Essenes where Jesus grew up studying the mystery schools, Mary Magdalene chronicles, *The Power of Myth* by Joseph Campbell, too many to list, and bejeweled globes, travelogues, and lion symbolisms. Thank you for always speaking your truth.

I request that my sacred scrolls, psalms, and original musicals be shared with the world. Therefore, I grant permission for my works to be published, recorded, and performed, understanding that they will be presented to reflect my artistic vision.

I designate my Blank Page Foundation as the recipient of any remaining funds in my estate. I wish for my legacy to benefit artists of all media and their creative endeavors.

Dearest fellow sojourners of truth, scribes of justice, and storytellers of freedom, I write this with a heavy heart, knowing the risks of pursuing truth and fair play would be at my peril. These sacred scrolls, journal entries, and love letters describe why I am no longer here. My grandmother wisely knew, 'We are the tales we tell ourselves.' Because of you, whom I may never meet in this world, I trust that Willow Rose, Apothecary, whom you will meet, and our voice, will not fall silent. That our beloved story will never be lost in time.

With that in mind, know that you are a Bridge Builder. Thank you for accepting my invitation to join this divine mission that transcends the confines of our pages. This quest to reverse the duplicitously wicked Cabal's clock, a countdown that will seal their atrocities in time, is essential. You have the power to illuminate the darkest corners of human experience. With every pen stroke, you cross the divide, foster wisdom, and breathe life into the stories that must be told. Wield your words not as weapons but as instruments of connection.

By penning noble narratives that reflect and connect humanity's beauty and complexity in a world that often feels fractured, your voice is a healing balm, offering solace to those who feel unheard or unseen. Seek out the stories of the marginalized, the silenced, and the forgotten; amplify their voices; share their struggles. Carry the torch of truth, peace, compassion, and empathy, and be faithful to the precious stories dwelling within you. The world is waiting for your voice. You belong to a worthy cause of exposing lies and empty promises of those wicked World Orderlies set to ravage joy, beauty, and compassion. Thank you for restoring stolen valor. I have hereunto set my hand and seal this day...

With unwavering hope,
Finnegan Padraig Kincannon

Love Letters
to Save the Future

Here's to the bridge-builders, the hand-holders,
the light-bringers, those extraordinary souls
wrapped in ordinary lives who quietly weave threads
of humanity into an inhumane world.
They are the unsung heroes in a world at war with itself.
They are the whisperers of hope that peace is possible.
Look for them in this present darkness.
Light your candle with its flame.
And then go. Build bridges. Hold hands.
Bring light to a dark and desperate world.
Be the hero you are looking for.
Peace is possible.
It begins with us.

~L. R. Knost

Chapter 1

My fellow Bridge Builder,

Welcome. With a prayer of truth surrounding us and synchronicity blessing us, our divine angels of traveling mercies go before us, beside us, behind us, and beneath us. Unfolding in the timeless spheres of transformation, we follow the rivers that weave through such elegantly extraordinary essences and the treacherous channels of deception. These exceptional experiences allow us to see through the smoke and mirrors of a duplicitously wicked world order.

A curtain of deception unexpectedly parted on a sublime summer's eve at the celebrated Oakwood County Club. From this departure onward, imagine yourself as an esteemed guest of the secreted soiree about to be unveiled and a bold Bridge Builder saving our precious world from the brink of destruction.

We are deep-diving into clandestine circles where conspiracies dwell, yet heroes and sheroes stand ready once dispatched. Driving into the exquisite Club, its environmental energy inspires joy to bubble up from within. The sweeping entrance evokes an ambiance of timeless elegance. Marked by an impressive archway bearing their two-hundred-year-old emblem, it is indicative of the remarkable history dwelling within. Entering through its old-world, ivy-covered stone walls between stately wrought iron fences, its majestic architecture exudes refinement.

Nestled in the foothills of a magnificent mountain range, it is encircled by meticulously manicured lawns that ripple out; they are velvet, verdant carpets whose vibrant flowerbeds burst with color. Tall, distinguished trees line the winding drive, their branches swaying gently in the breeze, creating a sense of tranquility and seclusion — an experience steeped in quaint charm.

The aristocratic club is a sanctuary for the elite, where the rich and powerful gather to socialize, relax, and indulge in the finer things in life. Underneath its ultra-sophisticated facade of luxury lurked an impromptu event shrouded with ominous secrets.

The club's intricate appurtenances and illustrious club's well-appointed accouterments are celebrated. Magnificently marbled floors, elaborate mirrors, and exquisitely sparkling chandeliers frame conversations among the elite and cast a warm glow across polished white oak tables. Perfectly appointed placements of shimmering dinnerware enhance the ornately woven wall tapestries.

Astonished by Oakwood's grandeur, looking up, you are struck by the high ceilings adorned with intricately hand-carved molding. The subtle play of precious gemstone lighting encourages prisms to cascade down the walls like jewels.

As you discover nooks filled with art and sculptures, a sense of wonder grows within you. Pausing, you admire a particularly striking piece and feel a spiritual connection to its craftsmanship; it speaks to your soul. In this hallowed space, a sense of deep gratitude washes over you as your desire to embrace beauty and delve into your creativity floods your spirit.

In this splendid space, you feel much more confident, a smile spread across your face, your senses are heightened, and the scent of fresh flowers mingles with the subtle fragrance of fine wood polish, creating a heady aroma that draws you further in. As your mood is elevated, it uplifts you from the everyday concerns of life into a realm where worries seem distant. When the glint of gold catches your eye, you experience the blessings that the outside world has faded.

Now, if only these hideaway halls could talk. Going back decades, the world would be utterly shocked to overhear this distinguished den's disturbing dialogues within these guarded chambers. When corrupt billionaires, mainly megalomaniacs, gather and exploit these opulent energies, weaving them into a dark and complicated tapestry of elaborate schemes, fortunes, and ill-gotten gains of absurd wealth are accumulated. It proved to be an unspeakable corruption that was one of the diabolical plots and obsolete patterns I came into this life to reveal and release.

With adages such as 'Saddle up, it is time to ride,' 'Spread your wings, let us fly,' and 'Now Boarding, a Freedom Flight is departing, leave your old baggage at the gate and prepare to BE Sublime.' Per my Gawni, this is an interactive quest to save our divine democracy.

During a time of profound transformation, we are ready to fly in the magnificent winds of change, tapping into layers of the esoteric, ancient wisdom of this Age of Aquarius. It is an incredible time when Pluto will unleash rebellion in the form of peace, pushing the river in the ways of wind and water. Known as Feng Shui's Period 9, it ushers in the blessings of passion, civil unrest, optimism, enthusiasm, luminosity, and clarity.

Lavish Cocoon

Oh, what a tangled web we weave
when we practice to deceive.

~Sir Walter Scott

Chapter 2

The sunset cast a fiery red and golden glow over the legendary Oakwood Country Club's luxurious lawns. Arriving in a black bullet-proof SUV, accompanied by his Marvel-Universe-looking beasts of bodyguards, was former Navy Seal, once shrewd attorney-at-law, and long ago a champion of the underserved was the prominent fourth generation, Grand Old Party, GOP Senator Malcolm Montgomery Blackwood.

In just two days, the Senator orchestrated this highly secretive event of madcap concealments. He secured the club's renowned Chef Isabella Toussaint and me, the head server. I am honored also to be the evening entertainer and the singing waiter for Broadway show tunes.

With Blackwood's prevailing persuasion, his cast of eight influential characters attending his covert dinner party was impressive. Each rich and famous attendee was dressed in their finest attire. Upon their arrival, they were discreetly shepherded into the ultra-chic, privileged, and private dining chamber. Blackhearted Blackwood (more about this well-earned term later) had crafted a seductive stage, a trap. Classical music floated through the secluded space, enveloping the selected invitees into a lavish cocoon.

Thematic, even cinematic centerpieces named "Garden of Eden" spoke of such sumptuous splendor. Lovely floral arrangements featuring chrysanthemum's, ranunculus, peonies, and dahlias mixed with fragrant herbs of thyme, mint, and basil overflowed from their hand-blown, ruffled glass vases. Delicate sweet pea and ivy tendrils cascaded over the edges. Their soft pastels of blush pink, lavender, and white, complimented by rich, vibrant greens, deceptively evoked serenity.

This starkly contrasted with Blackwood, who was seated confidently while captivating his audience with stories of bipartisan successes. His presence was as polished as the decor around him. Yet, beneath the senator's affable demeanor lay hidden secrets. His calculating eyes masked carefully cultivated respectability.

As he toasted the attendees with his signature Glenmorangie, the Lasanta Highland single-malt Scotch Whiskey, his gaze briefly strayed to the bay windows framing the silhouetted moonlit mountains. He was momentarily lost in memory of once being a presidential candidate and toast of the club. Not presently groveling for the puppet his party was paying to put in power, candidate Richard Ronald Tador.

His formidable Democratic rival was Genesis "Gen" Wentworth Wordsmith, my preferred candidate. It was time for a woman to be president; as someone born in the White House when her father was our American president, she is a former Civil Rights attorney, served as a Governor and then a Senator, and was once Secretary of State. She is highly qualified.

As head waiter, my job was to oversee the staff and serve the dais, the Senator's head table with two of his eight guests, Theodore 'Theo' Benjamin and Magnolia "Maggie" Mayfield Kensington, were seated.

The Senator knew this unprincipled couple were opportunists who would willingly accept all his duplicitous notions, so he sat them beside him. The recently wedded couple had received an extraordinarily generous gift from Maggie's billionaire father, Magnus Markham Mayfield, reportedly associated with organized crime. The gift was his right-wing, ultra-conservative WFTP radio, now a podcast, and his television network.

With the meteoric rise in dissatisfaction among fifty percent of Americans, not as the country of doers, overcomers, and believers but as cynics, shamers, and blamers, it would become Blackwood's favorite go-to platform. The culture shifted from those who chose to rise above, usually like the Phoenix, from the ashes of their past, where they learned valuable lessons, to a nation that wanted to burn down democracy.

Theo and Maggie were superficially rapt with interest and hung onto every one of Blackwood's sugar-coated words. Old Malcolm looked like a hungry wolf eager to devour his prey. Pull in those teeth, Grandma, you are salivating.

Unfortunately, people like the Senator, Theo, and Maggie often ignore servers like me. Oblivious of our presence until they require our help, shallow privilege, and imagined entitlements make them careless. It was part of the job, and I never took it personally. Indeed, these three were utterly unaware of me supplying them with delicious canapes and filling crystal flutes with Krug champagne. Dismissing me with a wave, not even bothering to look in my direction, turned out to be most fortuitous. Little did I know that being invisible would have significant benefits.

While standing at their beck and call, I inadvertently overheard Blackwood telling Maggie and Theo about his shocking plans, which radically and forever changed my life. More than its impact on me was the possibility of releasing this ominous plot to dismantle our fragile yet incredibly blessed democracy. I was speechless and even felt utterly betrayed. You will soon learn that Blackwood has a habit of shattering my world. This was surreal.

As in awakening from a nightmare, upon realizing what was happening in real time, my intense sense of responsibility to prevent these significant wrongs surfaced. The thought of Blackwood and his megalo-maniac billionaires perpetrating this scheme upon our nation was revolting.

Discreetly, I slipped my phone out of my shirt pocket from beneath my starched apron bearing the Oakwood crest. With the tap of an icon, I began recording their sinister conversation. Being readily ignored, I gathered evidence of their corruption, while Blackwood, Theo, and Maggie's arrogance was evident.

As their conversation became increasingly dark, my reaction to eavesdropping on Blackwood's evil plans to dissolve democracy became visceral. I could no longer contain my disgust. To avoid confronting them, I made a quick excuse to refill the coffee carafe. My God, this was devastating!

DANGEROUS TIMES

Treachery and violence are
spear points at both ends.
They wound those who resort to them
worse than their enemies.

~Emily Bronte

CHAPTER 3

Rushing to the club's kitchen, my heart pounded with every step. Almost bowling over two elderly members strolling the grounds, I resumed running after ensuring they were okay. Dashing into the gourmet galley, my eyes darted from side to side, adrenaline surging; I saw Chef Isabella and frantically thundered, *"My God, Treason, it is fricken' high treason, Senator Malcomb Montgomery Blackwood is committing sedition.*

Breathless, I continued, *"Chef, please listen to me. The evidence is on my phone; I recorded his every word. I have proof that this is more than a conspiracy theory; it is the real deal! Blackwood is plotting to dismantle our entire future. The world we once knew is being systematically undone."*

The chef's face was a canvas of confusion, her features etched with the sheer shock of my wild but true accusations. This claim was a crime of the highest order, not to be taken lightly, especially when it involved a man of the Senator's stature.

Chef Isabella, known as Izzy to her friends, including me, was more accustomed to my upbeat and witty nature, so this abrupt transformation into a raging madman was a jarring and disturbing sight — like a perfect storm in a once tranquil sea.

When I was hired three months earlier, Izzy and I quickly bonded. It was more than just a chance that we discovered we were distant cousins. As fellow foodies, music, and movie enthusiasts, we loved being Gen Z's. This was her third year at Oakwood's posh country club as the master chef, and she loved it there. Being highly sensitive to her loyalties, I asked,

"Izzy, you must admit that the air thickened with an odd sense of foreboding with tonight's clandestine dinner party. Am I right?"

I could see she was still trying to process my bizarre outburst; possibly, the unintended consequences of my actions were looming large. The potential danger of the situation hung in the air like a heavy fog, casting profound apprehension over the entire kitchen.

Izzy's voice quivered with disbelief, and her eyes were wide with the incredulity of my charge. She whispered to me, "*I can't believe this.*"

Izzy's anxious feelings enveloped her in a fear that underlined the seriousness of the situation. She placed her caring hands on my quaking shoulders and steered me to her private office. Her deep concern was evident. Worryingly, yet gently, she asked, "*What's going on, Mon Cheri? Senator Blackwood's secretive dinner falls under the Club's NDA we signed, which is exactly why they have an ironclad non-disclosure agreement. Do not repeat anything you think you may have overheard; its enormity could be catastrophic. Our silence will protect our jobs.*"

Catching her breath, she emphasized, "For the love *of God*, my *dearest Finn, Breathe! Sit tight, and I will be right back. I must explain to my staff, who are now gawking at you, that this is all a joke. Here, drink this chamomile tea.*"

Breathe? Well, okay, so I gulped in a small gasp of air, which temporarily soothed my acute anxiety. My mind then flickered back to the historical fiction my grandmother Gawni Grace, an Environmental Healer who decodes the Wheel of Time, has written. Her well-researched book, set in tumultuous 16th-century France, is the story of a brave protagonist, Willow Rose Toussaint, an Apothecary.

Willow must survive and thrive during a regime of tyrannical religious persecution, duplicitous political posturing, and shifting allegiances. Her plight and my current predicament feel like perfect parallels, which gave me a sudden jolt. I am registering the profound connection between Willow and my experiences, which have a divine connection.

Born in 1540 A.D., Willow is on an adventurous and dangerous mission to save our future. Will she live to fulfill her destiny? Now, the same sense of providence has been delivered to me. The future of democracy is at stake, intertwined with healing, miracles, and love.

In Willow's story, she is entangled in a wicked web of power woven by the ruling elite of her medieval timeline. The Catholic pope, jealous of her healing abilities, placed a lucrative bounty on her head. It is the first of the many rewards offered to eradicate those he called witches. Just how many witches were burned at the stake or drowned? None; they were innocent women who were healers and apothecaries who understood the medicinal herbs and potions to cure disease, fight infection, and comfort the dying. Can you imagine if anyone in today's business of Essential Oils is accused of heresy? It would be ludicrous.

Willow uncovered a plot that threatened to upend the monarchy, a conspiracy involving wealthy nobles who sought to manipulate the throne for their gain, and she faced relentless persecution.

Based on Blackwood's conversation, would this be my fate if I revealed its duplicitousness? The echoes of ancient and modern history resonated within my heart, reminding me that the fight for truth was imperative, regardless of the timeline.

Speaking of time, I must return to the gathering and resume the Universe's cloak-and-dagger assignment. As I left, I promised Izzy I would play the recording for her during tonight's routine teatime. She reminded me that two of Blackwood's esteemed guests, Amalie Avalon and Alexander "Alex" Lancaster Longwell, would formally introduce us at the get-together. I assured her I would calm down and regain my usual composure by then.

After hastily ensuring my phone was still in my pocket, I hugged Izzy and returned to the gourmet kitchen to grab a carafe of freshly brewed coffee. The outstanding Amalie and Alex are always a godsend. If it were not for their presence, Izzy would not even consider letting me return to the dinner gathering. Nor would she be here in America, as our Chef from France.

Before diving deep into Blackwood's pool of deceit, it is an honor to tell you more about our Izzy. We were amazed by our ancestral connection through Willow Rose Toussaint, Apothecary. Read on…

DEDICATION

Don't die with your music still in you.

~Wayne Dyer

CHAPTER 4

When Izzy received Senator Blackwood's last-minute reservation for eight influential power brokers, two of his entourage and himself, a total of eleven people, with only two days' notice, she jumped into action. She managed a whirlwind of tasks to ensure an exceptional dining experience. Initiating a menu highlighting her culinary skills that could be rapidly prepared was what she was known for. Izzy always aimed to balance sophistication and creativity by selecting a multi-course meal featuring seasonal ingredients to impress and pamper her guests.

Next, she coordinated with her kitchen staff, ensuring everyone was aligned, including delegating, sourcing, food preparation, and cooking tasks. Given short notice, she bought locally to secure the freshest ingredients, negotiating for prompt deliveries and ensuring everything arrived on time.

She also prepared the dining room set-up, interweaving the ambiance that suited the occasion best. This involves liaising with the front-of-house team to arrange for the perfect table settings, lighting, and decorations that reflect the country club's elegance, which includes personal touches, such as custom menus or place cards, making the guests feel special.

Timing is crucial, so she developed the evening's detailed timeline, ensuring that each course is served at the right moment and the experience has a seamless flow. There is no time to rehearse the sequence of service, but this is my area of expertise and where I shine.

Together, we oversaw the kitchen operations on dinner day, guaranteeing everything was thoroughly executed. We made sure to take the time to personally greet our influential guests, establishing rapport and making them feel valued. Ultimately, our goal is to create a memorable dining event that reflects Chef Isabella's famous cuisine while catering to the expectations of our high-profile clientele.

With her remarkable organizational skills and passion for cooking, Izzy transformed a last-minute reservation challenge into an opportunity to showcase her culinary artistry and unparalleled hospitality.

The guests were keenly aware of the important, albeit mysterious, discussions that would soon take place. Expectations also ran high with the promise of dining upon the celebrated young Chef Isabella Sophia Toussaint's sumptuous food. Even though secrecy enveloped the evening before the eavesdropped revelations unfolded, this dinner deepened silver-lined pockets of joy. I was reminded that life is a series of moments — each a chance to connect, explore, and celebrate the value of being together.

Now that you know more about Izzy's dedication to bringing blessings to the world, you can see how I believed she could partner with me. She is fully equipped to be pressed into boots on the battle-ground for freedom. Since the Mussolini and Hitler regimes murdered her maternal and fraternal great-grandparents, the populist effort to establish alt-right norms goes against her grain. She, like myself, is determined to keep these historical atrocities alive.

Dearest Bridge Builder, thank you for keeping an open mind and loving heart; we are moving onward. With this unexpected turn of events, seeing, well, in my case, hearing from behind the curtain, I am honored to answer this precious call. So much truth is being revealed about the attempt to hijack our future.

With gratitude, it is an interconnected weaving of practical theories, teachings, and traditions of patterns that beg to evolve. Discovering the blessings of ancient wisdom, intercultural enrichments, and historical wisdom, we write a future of pesticide-free foods, clean drinking water, and clear skies to support healthy bodies, minds, and spirits.

With the significant reset of the globe, Izzy, Willow, and I are serving as a guiding light in today's fast-paced world. The opportunity to delve deep into timeless truths, heartening personal growth, and self-discovery while addressing contemporary challenges is worthy. Blending profound insights with actionable strategies, we are inspired to envision a more peaceful and harmonious existence, empowered and encouraged to manifest these intentions.

As each page unfolds, let us explore our inner landscape, fostering a connection between the mystical and the mundane, ultimately revealing that the path to a transformed world begins within each one of us.

United to reveal Blackwood's intent on tearing apart our extraordinary country, couldn't people see that billionaires, oligarchs, megalomaniacs, and foreign influences were using people like Blackwood and candidate Tador to worm their way into our government and undermine Democracy? They did not even realize they were merely pawns; puppets being manipulated by puppet masters pulling their strings. Favors, finances, and flattery easily won them over. There is a universal clock that seeks to seal these atrocities into time, yet not on our watch.

Indeed, we are Bridge Builders of the past, present, and future, upholding the importance of a strong foundation that supports society's sacred structure. Let us erode old patterns that attempt to hold us hostage and cycle repeatedly; we are progressive, empathetic, and evolve humanity into its rightful place of peace, joy, and harmony.

INTRODUCTIONS

That perfect day, that magic moment
we are all waiting for, is right now.

~Kevin Griffin

To experience magical moments, when the Longwells are present, every moment is relished, and enchantment abounds. Alexander and Amalie Longwell are two of the eight power brokers in attendance and were pleased to have been invited. As robust Progressive's who believed or at least had hoped Blackwood was extending an olive branch to create a bipartisan community.

At the fated night's dinner, once the guests were seated, the handsome Alex stood up, tapped a silver spoon on the crystal champagne glass rim, and announced, *"Thank you, Senator Blackwood, for hosting this prestigious, albeit mysterious, gathering. I am grateful everyone here knows one another. I am honored to introduce our cherished friend, the highly acclaimed Master Chef Isabella "Izzy" Sophia Toussaint. Tonight, we have the pleasure of experiencing her exquisite culinary creations that have graced the tables of dignitaries and royalty alike. And, without further ado, may I present the magnificent Izzy."*

The Power of Friendship

*A friend may well be reckoned the
masterpiece of nature.*

~Ralph Waldo Emerson

CHAPTER 6

Stepping forward, Izzy humbly clasped her hands in appreciation, bowed, and said, "*Thank you, Mr. Longwell. The title of a highly acclaimed chef expresses the joy of my lifetime. Cooking is not just my profession; it illustrates my gratitude for the opportunity to nourish others and create lasting memories around the table.*

Each dish is crafted with care and creativity to bring people together. The blessings come from seeing you; my guests delight in the flavors and the generational stories behind each dish, making every meal a celebration of community, collaboration, and connection. I am grateful to have prepared tonight's cuisine.

It is also one of my most profound honors to share how, three years ago, the Longwells became my incredible benefactors. In a providential twist of fate, they made this French girl's childhood dream of becoming a Master Chef in America and a citizen of the United States a reality. We credit synchronicity for our destined, ever-so-divine relationship. Indeed, dreams do come true. Respectfully I thank you. Bon Appetit."

Amalie took the floor, wiping away tears, and recalled the fortuitous evening they dined at the Michelin 5-Star Le Merci Restaurant in Paris, where they discovered Izzy.

Amalie then announced she had another star to introduce, "Please *welcome our beloved Finnegan "Finn" Padraig Kincannon. Per Sabbatical, he is on loan to us from the University to compose his third musical. At 24, this talented young man is the esteemed recipient of Oakwood's generous annual scholarship. In addition, Alex and I are sponsoring his musical and are honored to be funding his Blank Page Foundation. Finn: please come up and tell us about yourself.*"

I thanked Amalie profusely for the opportunity to complete my Bachelor of Fine Arts degree. I am beyond grateful that Amalie and Alex are the prime sponsors of my musical *Myrtle Wood* and teammates on my charitable foundation.

Humbly, I shared how the Arts are deeply rooted in my sense of well-being and continue to ground me in personal growth. They saved my life! I am paying it forward by giving young people their voice to express themselves creatively, evolve their talents, and discover a greater sense of self-worth.

My musical Myrtle Wood is based on our current culture's suffering from grim epidemics that include mental health issues, eating disorders, OCD, and anxiety. They are each relevant, complex, and undoubtedly accelerated by social media. My message is, "With the 'Write' Help, Recovery is Possible!"

I was a patient at a world-renowned clinic that specialized in the treatment of a myriad of disorders, such as anorexia, bulimia, and morbid obesity. I am their poster boy, alive and well, and I can confirm that following proper systems can lead to a harmonious life. I fictionized patients' names and the facility to honor their NDA. Since I blended my fellow patients' challenges, it disguised any resemblances. It tells the courageous story of how we each find our way back to belonging.

"For that night's solo, I sang Stephen Sondheim's song, **No One is Alone** *from the* m*agnificent musical* **Into the Wood.**

> *"Mother cannot guide you*
> *Now you're on your own*
> *Only me beside you*
> *Still, you're not alone*
> *No one is alone. Truly,*
> *No one is alone."*

Upon finishing the song, I was given a robust round of applause. Amalie pulled Izzy and me to her heart and hugged us. She noted, *"Thank you. Having you two immensely talented and kind people with us tonight is truly an honor. Izzy and Finn, in your unique ways, you are catalysts for change, artistic visionaries who have added such a sweet touch of innocence and inspiration to our gathering. We are reminded of integrity's importance. I support your fresh voices, far-reaching visions, and mental, emotional, and physical health victories."*

The evening was pivotal to what was ahead of us.

PLOT THICKENS

The most beautiful people we have known are those who have known defeat, known suffering, known struggle, known loss, and have found their way out of the depths.

~Elizabeth Kubler-Ross

CHAPTER 7

E ven the clinking of crystal champagne glasses and soft murmurs of conversation could not disguise the underlying tension in the air. The guests' laughter rang hollow, whispers swirled, and the music took on a haunting quality.

The compelling impact of Oakwood Country Club's luxurious energy provided the perfect backdrop for this clandestine dinner. As the evening progressed, eerie shadows cast by flickering candlelight danced spookily across the walls, creating a sense of foreboding.

Our impeccably dressed staff, especially Izzy and I, who are usually attentive and polite, were tense and on edge. Nonetheless, as the night wore on, the guests dined on gourmet cuisine and sipped aged wines; their hushed voices delved into matters of state and strategy.

I observed how these beautiful people were in the circles of innovative, successful, and political influence. Privileged and private conversations were hidden behind a veil of luxury and exclusivity. Indeed, the plot thickened.

Beacons of Hope

*Be a guiding light, a safe harbor, a beacon of hope,
and a solid foundation for those around you.*

~Jennifer Gayle

Chapter 8

When the Longwells first approached Izzy about moving to America and considering the Oakwood Country Club's head chef position, they wrote her the following letter:

Dear Chef Isabella,

We hope you are doing well. As avid food enthusiasts and admirers of your incredible talent, we want to express our appreciation for your culinary artistry. Your innovative dishes and passion for cooking have made a mark in the culinary world, and we do not doubt that you are a rising star.

We are writing to you with a unique proposition you may consider. As a couple living in the storied Oakwood Country Club community, we have followed your journey at the Parisian's Five-Star Michelin restaurant Le Merci from afar. Your imaginative creativity and commitment to excellence continuously inspire us.

Oakwood Country Club is known for its vibrant food scene and welcoming atmosphere that embraces culinary innovation. Your presence here would elevate our local dining experiences and provide a supportive environment in which to grow and share your talents further. Your skills and vision would resonate beautifully in our community.

We understand that moving is a significant decision, but Oakwood would be an ideal place for you to expand your culinary horizons. We would be thrilled to assist you in any way possible during this transition, from helping you find a suitable, cherished space to dwell in to connecting with local suppliers who share your passion for quality ingredients.

Please remember that this invitation comes from a place of admiration and respect for your work. We would be honored to have the opportunity to enjoy your dishes in person and to support your journey as you continue to rise in the culinary world. We look forward to the possibility of welcoming you to the prestigious Oakwood Country Club and witnessing the magic you will undoubtedly bring to our community. We hope you will consider our offer.

An article about us from Time Magazine is enclosed to help you appreciate our sincere interest in all things progressive, including your future with the prestigious Oakwood and our dedication to assisting others.

In this article titled "Beacons of Hope," the dynamic duo of Amalie Avalon and Alexander "Alex" Lancaster Longwell's story unfolds as a modern-day fairy tale. Both hailing from humble beginnings, they climbed the corporate ladder, carving out a niche in the tech and finance sectors.

Amalie, a brilliant coder and entrepreneur, founded a ground-breaking tech startup focused on renewable energy solutions. With Alex's sharp instincts and keen financial acumen, he transformed a struggling investment firm into a powerhouse by prioritizing sustainable energy investments.

Their paths crossed at a conference on energy innovation, where their shared vision for a better world sparked an instant connection. Together, they launched a philanthropic initiative for budding innovators and entrepreneurs.

As their influence grew, so did their commitment to philanthropy. They established the Longwell Arts & Innovative Foundation, which supports various causes, including educational advances, artists, environmental conservation, and mental health awareness. Their efforts have not gone unnoticed, earning them accolades and recognition in numerous publications. Their love story, marked by passion and purpose, has captured the public's imagination.

They have graced the covers of prestigious magazines such as Forbes, where they were featured as pioneers of the new philanthropic class, and ours, which named them among the 100 Most Influential People for their innovative approach to combining business with social responsibility.

Vanity Fair showcased them in a special issue dedicated to power couples, highlighting their glamorous lifestyle yet down-to-earth values and commitment to making a difference. They have even appeared in Rolling Stone and National Geographic magazines, which covered their contribution to green energy.

Amalie and Alex often appear in the media, discussing the importance of sustainable business practices, social responsibility, and the impact of philanthropic work. Their timeless tale is romantic and is an ambitious, shared dream of creating a brighter future; they are bridge builders, inspiring others to follow in their footsteps. Together, they are not just a power couple but a beacon of hope and change, proving that wealth can be a force for good in the world."

To your highest best,
Amalie & Alex

Indeed, Izzy's wondrous body of work and faith opened the door to her date with Destiny. As a miracle child, she believed in the power of synchronicity.

POWER OF THE WORD

Be impeccable with your word.

~Don Miquel Ruiz

Chapter 9

Dear Bridge Builder,

Because of the recordings of Blackwood, I am writing to you as one of a select few who will realize the importance of what I was destined to unravel. These letters to you, beloved family, treasured friends, and to our luminous future are words, testimonials, and intentions that will endure long after the dust settles.

To ensure that the truth is not lost to time and that the lessons learned are not buried beneath the consequence of how silence, evil alliances forged, and betrayals will lead to a reckoning that must be revealed. Here I am, laying bare the intricacies of a world that thrives on deception and ambition. Yet, I still believe in goodness, compassion, and honesty.

This is not merely my astonishing story but a cautionary tale exploring the fragile nature of democracy, power, and trust. It is also a homage to those who were lost along the way.

Reflecting on that fateful night that forever changed my destiny, I am astonished at what I overheard — those hushed conversations, a dance whose choreography horrified me, unwittingly drawing me into a gloomy world where every word dripped with ulterior motives.

Thank you for being a Bridge Builder. I implore you not to compromise your values or be reduced by fear, anger, or blame. This journey called life is not for the faint of heart; it requires believing in diligence, bravery, love, and an intentional focus on beauty, bliss, and blessings. Indeed, we are the tales we tell ourselves. The power of the word is magnificent, miraculous, and majestic.

PASSION

Once something is a passion,
the motivation is there.

~Michael Schumacher

CHAPTER 10

Senator Blackwood was a man of power and influence, but behind his polished veneer lurked a darker side. Known for his underhanded tactics and shady dealings, Blackwood had amassed a fortune by manipulating his associates by threatening to reveal scandalous information and backroom deals. He was known for being ruthless and cunning, willing to do whatever it took to maintain his grip on power.

The luxury location is indeed lavish with amenities and breathtaking views, making it a symbol of success and sophistication. Blackwood dangled the allure of rubbing shoulders with high society and influential figures, suggesting that aligning with his devious plans would lead to additional wealth and advancement opportunities. Moreover, he will use the Oakwood Country Club to create an artificial façade, an appeal of entitlement.

Hosting events and meetings in such an elegant setting fosters a sense of exclusivity and belonging. Overall, the affluent environment is a powerful tool to entice potential supporters into their corrupt plans, leveraging the charm of wealth, power, and privilege.

Blackwood's guests include political journalist Evelyn "Eve" Eden Everhart, his damage control person. He does not leave home without her. Because I have already done my research, I will give you her back story, which underlines how cunning Blackwood is to surround himself with his believers.

But first, I am introducing you to another member of his team, the noted former environmental advocate who turned lobbyist, the handsome Jasper "Jax" Joseph, who is always two steps behind them.

In his early thirties, Jax's curly dark hair, deep-set green eyes that carry the weight of his conscience, and chiseled jawline draw compliments.

He initially built his career on a solid foundation of principles, driven by a passion for sustainability and a desire to protect the environment. He worked tirelessly to promote green initiatives, advocating for policies that preserve natural resources and combat climate change. His field of expertise was agriculture. He proved the soils were over-fertilized by poisonous chemicals and devoid of nutrients, and the time for a new way of farming had come. Although his passion project continues to be aquaponics, after years of dedicated work, Jax grew disillusioned with the environmental sector's slow progress and bureaucratic hurdles.

Seeking a more immediate impact, he transitioned into lobbying, believing he could still effect change from within the system. He secured a lucrative position at a powerful firm that promised to align corporate interests with environmental goals. However, as he settled into this new role, he discovered that his firm engaged in a corrupt scheme that exploited vulnerable communities under the guise of green development projects.

Jax grappled with a moral dilemma as he began to connect the dots. He was torn between his desire to expose the corruption and protect his career, which came with financial security and social status. Jax is intelligent and resourceful, using his charm and persuasive skills to navigate the treacherous waters of corporate politics. He gathered evidence discreetly, using his insider knowledge to document the illegal activities without drawing attention to himself.

To reveal the plot without jeopardizing his career, Jax employs a strategy of anonymous whistleblowing. He carefully crafted a detailed report outlining the corruption, ensuring it is backed by solid evidence and testimonies from those affected. He contacted a trusted journalist, Sheamus Samuel Kilgore, known for brilliant investigative reporting, and provided him with the information through a secure channel that masks his identity.

Simultaneously, Jax was wise to build alliances with other lobbyists and environmental advocates who shared his concerns, subtly raising awareness of the issue within the industry while maintaining his facade.

Jax's journey was marked by internal conflict as he walked a fine line between ambition and integrity. He struggled with the fear of retaliation but finds strength in his commitment to justice. His desire to protect innocent people and restore his sense of purpose drives him to take calculated risks, leading him to redemption in the face of corruption. At just the right time, Jax resigned from the fake Eco Firm he managed to bring down. They were forced to pay restitution for their white-collar crimes.

Jax knew the Senator participated in numerous secret swindles. Yet, he was never publicly associated with them except for a scandalous land fraud scheme. Due to his political influence, he managed to skirt justice. Jax secured a position on Blackwood's team to reveal his corruption. The sky was a perpetual shade of gray, a testament to the thick pollution over the cities. Corporations ruled the land, their influence seeping into every crevice of daily life. Jax was committed to his quest to create a better future.

Just Who Is Finnegan Padraig Kincannon?

The measure of a man is what he does with power.

~Plato

Chapter 11

1 was honored to read a letter of recommendation from the Dean of Fine Arts to the Longwells regarding my potential employment at Oakwood. She was kind enough to send me a copy as follows:

Dear Mr. and Mrs. Longwell,

In response to your letter of endorsement for Finnegan Kincannon, who is being considered for Oakwood Country Club's head waiter position, I am honored to provide a glowing recommendation. As his Fine Arts professor, I have been blessed to witness many aspects of Finn's vast talent pool.

Serving with kindness, he is an enthusiastic performer who genuinely engages with people, cares about others, and enjoys enriching conversations. This makes him well-liked among his peers, professors, patrons, and co-workers. With every interaction, he focuses on making others feel seen and appreciated.

With his theatre background, I can see him gracefully yet robustly bringing to the job the energy required of a head server. He is keen on self-talk, constantly reminding himself that he has been trained for this good life and is always in the right place at the right time, synchronicity.

With his sky-blue eyes, Finn's striking presence captures the essence of deep oceans, reflecting warmth and undeniable intensity. Your members and guests will be impressed that his tousled blonde hair adds an effortless charm to his overall look, framing a face that blends youthfulness and mature depth.

When not taking orders or serving tables, he is immersed in his creative passions as a composer and an actor. He pours his soul into every note and draws inspiration from life's complexities. Undoubtedly, he is resolved to transform his challenges into something meaningful. The pursuit of his dreams is fueled by a desire to convey emotions and tell stories that resonate deeply with audiences.

As his professor, I see that he is entrenched in thoughts about the intricacies of character development or the nuances of musical composition. He analyzes situations from multiple perspectives, enriching his artistry with layers of value.

Balancing work demands with fervent ambitions, Finn is committed to discovering wisdom in life's ordinary and extraordinary aspects. He encounters beauty every day. I can highly recommend Finn as an employee of Oakwood Country Club. If you have any further questions, feel free to contact me.

Sincerely,

Judith J. Emerson
Director of Fine Arts

The Garden of Eden
Paradise Lost, Or Was It?

All is not lost, the unconquerable will
and study of revenge, immortal hate,
and courage never to submit or yield.

~John Milton

Chapter 12

honoring the symbolic centerpieces while sensing the noticeable tensions, I drew a strong parallel to the current political environment.

Blackwood was on his best behavior while on the politicking trail for billionaire celebrity, the Republican hopeful Richard Ronald Tador, as a never-before-government official, much less in the position of president.

R. R. Tador, an entertainer, is running against a well-respected, highly experienced, and former women's rights attorney, formidable Democratic Senator Genesis Winifred Wentworth Wordsmith, for the highest office in our country: President.

In retrospect, with the tables graced by thematic centerpieces named the Garden of Eden, I was struck by the connections to what I now know was a provocative, almost doomsday choice. Writing my legacy in early October, the rumors of overturning the 50-year ruling of Roe v. Wade are more than tall tales. We shall see.

Although Eve's story is interpreted through the lens of patriarchy, it is rooted in the biblical narrative of the Book of Genesis. I pray you are not lost in this segment and stay open to the correlation between Genesis, the candidate, and the Old Testament, equivalent to our culture's changing times.

As it was interpreted, Eve is created from Adam's rib and becomes the first woman in this narrative. They live in paradise, where their every desire is fulfilled. God prohibited them from eating the fruit in the middle of the garden, known as the Tree of Good and Evil.

In traditional interpretations, Eve is blamed for humanity's fall from grace. This fault has been perpetuated through centuries of patriarchal narratives that portray her as the origin of sin and disobedience. The implications of this story have often been used to justify female subjugation and reinforce patriarchal structures, casting women as temptresses of low morals and bearers of humanity's shortcomings.

However, in a more nuanced reading of the story, there is an alternative perspective on Eve's actions. Instead of viewing her as merely the instigator of sin, one could argue that Eve's choice to eat the fruit symbolizes a quest for knowledge and enlightenment. In this light, her decision represents a courageous step towards self-awareness and understanding, qualities that are often celebrated in a matriarchal framework.

By eating the fruit of the Tree of Knowledge, Eve gains insight into the nature of good and evil, which signifies a profound awakening. This act of seeking knowledge is interpreted as challenging the status quo, which may have been threatened by a matriarchal society that values wisdom, intuition, and inter-connectedness.

In this version, the patriarchal narrative's fear of Eve's wisdom could reflect a broader anxiety about women's potential to disrupt established power dynamics. The expulsion from Eden can be seen as a punishment and a means of controlling and suppressing feminine wisdom and intuitive knowledge that the patriarchal order found threatening. This scenario has played out since the beginning of time.

And dearest Bridge Builder, I'm reminded to review and revisit old, cherished stories through the lens of a new paradigm. My God, what if a man had taken that first bite? Oh, Hail Humanity, Wisdom pours forth from his greatness. A monument of the highest of virtue would be sculpted, forged next to the tree, and celebrated through-out history from that date onward.

INTO THE ABYSS

*Into the Abyss, where darkness meets destiny,
the uncharted journey of courage and resilience begins
as we navigate the depths of uncertainty to discover
the light within ourselves that guides us through.*

~Sharyn G. Jordan, Storyteller

Chapter 13

When I returned to the opulent dining room with the carafe and cups, I was mindful of Izzy's wise words of caution, which echoed in my mind. The dangers of revealing anything said between Blackwood and his guests was tantamount to being fired. Izzy had become my dear friend, a person whom I would never want to wound or intentionally harm. Yet, a misstep on my part could negatively impact her stellar career.

Confidently, I moved around the luxurious dining room, refilling the wealthy guests' empty cups of coffee. Everyone greeted me respectfully and kindly except for Blackwood and the Kensington power couple. With Blackwood's entitled attitude, I was grateful he did not acknowledge my presence; letting me slip unseen into the shadows was perfect. I used this opportunity to listen carefully and continue recording them.

At this point in the gathering, Blackwood reminds his invitees of his impressive military background and lengthy political service record. This is an overt attempt to make him appear trustworthy. However, he is also known to be ambitious to a fault.

Years ago, his lofty Presidential aspirations fell flat. It was a well-known fact that his running mate was a poor choice. When he threw him under the bus, he was shocked. And yet, he stands promoting another political figure, a nominee who has never respected him and continues disparaging his character.

Knowing Blackwood was a party loyalist and genuinely believed that he and his cronies could corral this overt narcissist, their presidential candidate who thinks he should be king, was in and of itself highly paradoxical.

My awareness sharpens as Blackwood engages in a clandestine conversation with Maggie and Theo. With their collective power, these guests have the potential to alter the world's balance and mold and model history through their decisions and influence.

Lost in my thoughts, I almost missed the arrival of dessert. It was ideal timing and brought me back to earth. Serving Izzy's spectacular Chocolate Truffle Torte brightened the atmosphere. With the guests' every sumptuous bite, its chocolaty base melted in their mouths; it was a pure balance of bitterness and sweetness if only the room's mood could replicate.

Unpleasant feelings of mounting pressure continued to simmer in the room, and I could not help but wonder if it would reach a boiling point. Thinly veiled by cheerfulness, their suspicions were evident in their unease as their carefully chosen words added to the evening's suspense. Whispers of Blackwood's hidden agenda circulated between the two couples, thickening the charged environment. They were suspicious and would soon be shocked.

Blackwood's web of espionage, sabotage, and corrupt arbitrage had long been underway. He, too, was a pawn of a sinister Cabal of Corruption. Their plots would attempt to misshape the fate of our nation and alter the course of history. Blackwood and his billionaire club's plan to steal and manipulate the upcoming presidential election was diabolical. The tension in the room was so thick you could cut it with a knife. Oh yes, it was indeed warranted.

Even though Blackwood already knew the enticing incentives of corrupt carrots he would dangle in front of these power brokers, the question remained: Could any of them be *brought* into his world-changing scenario, as in *bought* into?

Secrets Revealed

Three may keep a secret if two of them are dead.

~Benjamin Franklin

Chapter 14

When Blackwood bid Theo and Maggie good night, he took leave to be chauffeured home in the club's elite, well-guarded section of mansions. He would not yet return to his upscale Washington D.C. brownstone; he still had more wining and dining to do.

Quietly, I stood in the shadows of the dining room for what seemed forever when, finally, Theo and Morgan felt safe enough to speak aloud about going along with Blackwood's plan. Wisely, I also recorded it. Once I heard them depart, I breathed a deep sigh of relief.

Amidst a whirlwind of emotions, I found solace in my lifelong commitment to serving the underserved, defending justice, believing in the Constitution, and loving my country. My moral compass was my guiding north star as I navigated this uncharted path. I trusted it to lead me past any turbulence I may encounter. Plus, having the ancient wisdom of overcoming all adversity in my soul lent itself to this quest.

Intentionally living a life of creative fulfillment dispels the illusion that money buys happiness and power gives a person joy. These blessings can only come from within, a belief I held dear and one that guided my every action.

I was silently unraveling the high-stakes conspiracy upon which I had stumbled. The weight of this discovery pressed heavily on my heart. As I pieced together the fragments of their plan — an elaborate scheme to manipulate an upcoming election involving foreign influences, bribery, and blackmail — the gravity of what I'd just overheard and recorded was surreal.

As a deep thinker, I considered my fate and the implications of this dark evening on my future. From an elevated consciousness, I delved deeply into my Irish Grandmother, Grace Gayle Kincannon's infinite belief systems of positivity, leaning into gratitude, and the importance of trusting history inspired my stream of thoughts with a wisdom only a philosopher could match.

She taught me the importance of synchronicity, which means we were always in the right place and time. This truth is based on Carl Jung's theory that no random circumstances exist. This experience was most certainly one of synchronicity.

I considered how the serendipitous interplay of events reflects the interconnectedness of the inner and outer worlds and transcends the traditional notions of causation. When living intentionally, life echoes a much more prosperous and purposeful pattern. This practical yet divinely spiritual reality seamlessly connects the inner and outer worlds.

Reflecting upon my grandmother's historical fiction novel, I consider life's supernaturalness a natural process. Her book's topical relevance weaves itself into my present dilemma. Indeed, corrupt powers are ever-present throughout time and are constantly attempting to rule the world.

Contemplating these truths, a feeling of destiny swept through me. In a flash, I felt an innate connection to something more significant than myself — as if everything in my life had finally fallen into place. With a rush of inspiration, celestial energies propelled me forward. Indeed, synchronicity was present, and I knew what I must do.

Then, out of nowhere, I recalled my grandmother telling me about Edna Ferber's epic novel and the subsequent 1950s film *Giant*. The sweeping story of affluent yet indifferent Texas oil barons, mistreatment of immigrant workers, avarice, racism, and classism was controversial. Seeing the blockbuster movie at age eight, starring Elizabeth Taylor, Rock Hudson, and James Dean, made such an impact that she knew she was here to serve the underserved. So am I!

These recollections eliminated any reluctance I might have had to play the menacing recording for Izzy. The Senator's treasonous tactics were wicked, and I knew I would reveal his tactics, as well as those of the dictator, who is a con artist. They had tapped into the populist trend of fear, anger, and, sadly, general unhappiness. Their bullying, blame, and shame rhetoric was disparaging yet effective.

When Izzy hears these shocking conversations, I trust she will willingly be my accomplice in this quest for fair play. She has taken the initiative to make her life one of value and on purpose. Having a purpose in life is like having a guiding star; it provides direction, motivation, and a sense of fulfillment. Her career and purpose were the same, as was mine. Refining our gifts, experiencing personal growth, and contributing to the world ignite our passion. Each day becomes an opportunity to take steps into the journey, becoming incredibly rewarding.

In a moment of extraordinary intuition, my recent interest in Catholicism and its contradictory history, plus my searching for and finding our Irish heritage, my grandmother's book brilliantly flashed before my eyes. An ancient Celtic Knot emerged. This was not a mere coincidence but a confirmation of synchronicity.

Elegance of Isabella

Elegance is the only beauty that does not fade.

~Audry Hepburn

Chapter 15

Anticipating her nightly teatime with Finn, Chef Isabella briskly oversaw the closing duties of her kitchen staff. Izzy is the devoted daughter of talented French artist Sebastian Toussaint and the fascinating Italian actor, beautiful Sophia Isabella Rossi, whose silver screen presence is mesmerizing. Sabastian was known worldwide for his evocative paintings that captured the essence of joy, love, and passion.

Commissioned to paint Sophia's portrait for an upcoming movie was a date arranged by the universe. The moment they set eyes upon one another; sparks were ignited. It was magical. Sophia and Sabastian's radiant love story in romantic Paris was a cinematic masterpiece. Their deep connection transcended time.

They married in a fairy-tale wedding ceremony in Claude Monet's celebrated gardens of Giverny in the devoted company of their family and fellow artisans. These sacred soul mates were grateful to have found one another.

After ten years of blissful marriage, they wanted to share their profound love with a child. Sophia took time off from her acting career and began writing. Sebastian permanently relocated his studio to Paris and became involved in the fascinating restoration process of historical photography.

Their dedicated parenthood journey proved challenging, uncertain, and full of heartache. For years, their ongoing attempts were futile. By the time the Toussaint's were well into their forties, they were still childless, yet neither ever gave up hope.

Amazingly, on Valentine's Day 1989, with their emotions ranging from excitement to gratitude to cautious optimism, the extraordinary news of a successful conception brought them overwhelming joy. Isabella Francesca, their cherished Izzy, was born the following November 18. She was the love that filled their lives. As they poured their passion into her, Isabella, fondly nicknamed Izzy, experienced the tremendous joys of being loved and the infinite blessings of loving others.

Growing up, Izzy adored her father's mama Grand'Mere, Madame Camille Toussaint, a French Le Cordon Bleu graduate affectionately known as her Mimi. Izzy relished Mimi's childhood stories, who regaled her with a magnificently magical life as a young girl in pre-World War France. Of the horrors she experienced, yet the enduring strength she discovered within her soul while secretly resisting the Nazi occupation of her beloved country.

As a Master Chef, Izzy is a true culinary queen. Her eyes light up when she speaks about her craft, and her melodic accent — a blend of French lilt and Italian warmth — infuses her words with passion and charisma. She embodies a perfect blend of style, sensuality, and creativity, leaving an indelible mark on those privileged to experience her artistry. Izzy exudes elegance that draws respectful attention wherever she goes.

Her warm olive skin is a perfect canvas for expressing her vibrant heritage, which blends the French Riviera's breezy charm with Italy's enthusiastic spirit.

Standing at 5'7", her striking features include high cheekbones and a delicate jawline, giving her an air of sophistication. Her eyes are dark pools of violet-blue seas, holding secrets and stories that sparkle with intelligence and humor.

Framed by thick, long lashes that enhance their captivating depth, she draws people in with a glance. Her long, silk-like black hair cascades down her back in gentle waves, catching the light with hints of indigo. She often styles it in elegant chignons or allows it to flow freely, emphasizing her refined taste and carefree spirit.

Her skilled and agile hands transform simple components into extraordinary symphonies of flavors, a true testament to the beauty and artistry in her work.

Still in disbelief at Finn's accusations, Izzy was comforted that she would discover more tonight during her and Finn's nightly teatime. She was also soothed by the intense aromas of Herbes de Provence's fragrant bouquet, a blend of thyme, rosemary, basil, and marjoram that soothed her senses.

She ran her hands over her Le Creuset cast iron pots and French skillets, causing them to sway into one another lightly. Their musical chimes were the perfect rhythmic backdrop that grounded and calmed her.

Retiring to her cozy office was a welcome relief from the evening's unusual and unnerving drama. She flicked on the switch to power up her fairy lighting. The strands were strung all along her fireplace, whose illumination ran sideways and were continuously weaved into two bookshelves flanking the hearth. Adjacent were two thriving, six-foot-tall Money Tree plants.

Setting out a cherished tea set, which her mother had gifted her upon leaving France three years ago, was a privilege. These elegant cuppas were two treasures that survived her maternal great-grandmother, Isabella "Bella." Mussolini's Fascist Regime destroyed her once-wealthy estate. This lovely tea service was a tangible link to her lineage, to which she owes a debt of gratitude for living her luminous life, one she dearly loves. She was deeply appreciative of their sacrifices.

TEATIME

It is time to spill the tea.

~The Home Whisperer

Chapter 16

At tonight's teatime, I will acquaint Izzy with guests such as Jax and Eve, who she will not know, and other non-Oakwood members, such as bestselling author Charlotte Winifred and her husband, William "Will" Winston Wycliff.

The possible fallout of my treasonous claim could cast a dark cloud of uncertainty over the rest of my life. The very fabric of my world was unraveling, leaving me in a state of profound unease.

Unbeknownst to Izzy, I have a history and personal vendetta of profound intensity against Blackwood, who unforgivably betrayed my dad and our family. This was a searing vengeance from a personal tragedy, an agonizing emotional wound created by Blackwood's selfish decisions and actions.

Seeing the Senator after all these almost twenty years was eerie enough. I was grateful he did not recognize the six-year-old boy whose life he destroyed. The realization that I was now experiencing the exact unexpected fate of my father made me wonder about repeating familiar patterns of breaking Karmic codes. Would I also encounter Dad's same mental health challenges? I harbored this fear all my life; it haunted me. However, I have learned that when irrational thoughts arise, I tell myself, "*Delete, delete, delete.*

Izzy would soon learn of the emotional wounds created by what I discovered were at the behest of Blackwood's illicit and greedy actions regarding the Sherwood Behavioral Campus.

In the legend of Robin Hood, I would have been the hero giving the spoils of the rich to the poor. Blackwood was the villainous King who taxed the poor and gave to the rich. Once Izzy learns of this travesty, I hope she will become my Maid Marian.

When I finally arrived at the club's kitchen, I was calm. Even so, Izzy's maternal instinct kicked in, and she hugged me, asking, "*Are you okay?*"

Smiling, I reassured her, "*I am better, but my legs feel like rubber, and my stomach is churning.*"

I had taken my time walking to our nightly teatime. To get out of my head, I stood under the canopy of twinkling stars that cast a soft glow over the manicured grounds. A curvilinear path lent an air of enchantment to the jasmine covered porticoes, which found me inhaling their exquisite fragrances, a balm to my heart. Halting briefly, I considered the tranquility of the garden's three-tiered fountain, whose melodic waters gently trickled over a scalloped reservoir — it was even more medicine.

The recording on my phone was the legend of Blackwood's evil plot to upend the world I once knew. Since I had already devised a plan to secure its proof, I would seek out an investigative journalist and give a copy of my recording to the FBI. It was time to bring Izzy into this loop of grave importance.

Thinking about how to tell her of my twenty-year history with Blackwood made my head spin. It drove my motives beyond the political mayhem I had stumbled into. The connection between the tragedy of losing my father at the age of 26, who had mysteriously disappeared for a year and then died of mental health complications, possibly by way of suicide or even by murder. All I can do is tell her what I know to be factual, which I call the truth loop.

We are entering an era of major transformation, an entirely new way of being. In times of such significant change, we must discover the wealth of wisdom from within, evolve, and learn to be observers. We will decode the patterns of repeatedly high-stakes phases, ages, and stages that repetitively recycle and are replayed until they are finally broken and rewoven. I knew there was a strong connection between then and now.

This experience has a riveting medieval-era correlation that could even act to inform and reform our profound system of democracy and Lady Liberty's functions. Had I stumbled into a raucous wheel of time spinning towards a preordained destiny already set in motion? I do not accept that; we always have free will and let us consciously select our purpose even though fate often calls us first. Ah, let us choose wisely my dear Bridge Builders.

Like Father, Like Son

The apple does not fall far from the tree.

~Ralph Waldo Emerson, 1839

CHAPTER 17

"*Izzy, I have something to tell you before we listen to the daunting Blackwood recordings. You know, I have never fully recovered from the loss of my dad, Finnegan Padraig 'Paddy' Kincannon. I've been thinking a lot about him lately.*" Thankfully, my voice was steady but was still laced with emotion.

She sighed, compassion etched on her features. After a lengthy silence, she assured me she was my trustworthy friend and would be honored to hear anything on my mind. In gratitude, she offered me a choice of Lavender, Chamomile, or Ginger Peach tea. I opted for the latter with honey.

Izzy prepared a tray with her cherished tea service, a pot of organic honey, and a basket of freshly baked croissants. In a vase in her garden, fresh pink roses wafted through the atmosphere with pure love. Her cozy, private office was a refuge.

We settled into our familiar chairs. With soft jazz music playing in the background, I slipped off my shoes and relaxed for the first time. After a moment, I took a deep breath, preparing to lay bare a story that, even after twenty years, still brought me shame and even guilt for not having yet resolved or vindicated my dad's death. The best way to tell her my sincere story was to read her a letter my dad wrote me right before his death. I cleared my throat and began as follows:

Dearest Son,

You are in my prayers. Thinking of your sunny smile, infectious laughter, and precarious nature is a blessing. Life has been a long journey and has not unfolded in the ways I once thought it would. Even though I have not been in your life as much as I wished, you are forever in my heart.

Despite my ongoing struggles with mental, physical, and financial stability, I trust these letters will help you to know me. If you read this, I will have passed from this world and am well on my way to the next role in the soul's journey. I will get to that timeless wisdom later. For now...

I hope this letter finds you in peace, far removed from the chaos that has enveloped my mind for years. I want to share with you the struggles I faced, not to burden you, but to help you understand the darkness that sometimes envelops us and how it can twist our hopes into despair. For too long, I fought against the shadows that crept into my mind, thoughts that whispered lies and fears that suffocated my spirit. I tried to be strong for you, to shield you from the pain that clawed at my heart. But in that struggle, I found a purpose I hope you will carry forward when I am gone.

Your grandmother, my mother, has instructions to give you my journal entries and these letters, one at a time and only upon my death. I know it seems at odds with my life; however, I am at peace.

In retrospect, the most progress I made in championing my challenges fell apart due to a broken and outdated mental health system that failed not only me but thousands more in need. For me, what the medical community calls Bipolar Disorder is something altogether different, at least in my case.

My son, I hope you can help me set my record straight. First, you must know that I have proof of why the state-run mental health facility I relied on was illegally shut down for profit. Senator M. M. Blackwood is one of the persons responsible for the closures. It is sickening.

While waiting for hours in Sherwood's Admissions, my nerves were frayed, and I needed a smoke. Seeing everyone was busy processing others, I walked down the hall and found an unlocked office. I was about to light my cigarette when I heard the doorknob turn; I hunkered under a large desk. Shielded by the privacy panel, I peered through a slot and saw two men entering.

I recognized one of them as Blackwood, the ribbon cutter at Sherwood's Grand Opening. I did not know the other person who handed the Senator a large envelope stuffed with money. They shook hands, and he confirmed that this facility would be privatized within the month.

My heart dropped. True to Blackwood's promise, I was back on the streets, homeless again, within three weeks. I was too ashamed to reach out and wandered for weeks that turned into months.

With love,
Dad

Izzy's compassion for my dad's long-held anguish was heartfelt. This experience is not just the fire of anger that burns inside me but a raging inferno that fuels my every action. Although I never knew my dad as well as I wanted, he has always been in my heart.

I told her I vividly remembered how grateful and relieved my family was when Dad was accepted into the state-of-the-art Sherwood Behavioral Campus, SBC, a state-supported program he qualified for.

It answered our fervent prayers, especially those of my six-year-old self. Yet, within a month of his being accepted and admitted, Dad was mysteriously released; he disappeared and was later found dead. His catastrophic death was devastating.

Years ago, my grandmother told me that Dad witnessed the corrupt Blackwood accepting a bribe to shut down Sherwood as a public facility and move it into privatized for-profit care. Investors, insurance agents, lobbyists, and big pharma companies paid politicians tremendous sums to do this nationally. This was not a minor fraud.

"*Oh, Izzy, was my overhearing the crooked Blackwood and his schemes synchronistic? Like Father, like Son, what were the odds? Slim to none!*"

Thoughtfully, Izzy replied, "*Finn, I'm positive this is more than a coincidence. You have encouraged me to trust the universe to answer our questions. As shocking as it is, isn't this the proof you have always sought?*"

"*Thank you, Izzy, you are so perceptive. When the SBC's assisted programs shifted to being a more lucrative, privatized system, Paddy was released. It's devastating results crushed his hopes of recovery. Without access to the necessary housing assistance, counseling, and medical care, my dad spiraled further into mental and emotional decline.*

Growing up, I was told bits and pieces of Dad's tragic challenges. Rooted within me, I must admit, was a fear that branched out into every part of my life. Did the apple fall not so far from the tree? What if my mental health fell into the same despair?

Thanks to the support of my mother and both sets of grandparents, being active in theatre and attending university was my therapy. I became determined to find meaning in my struggles and sought redemption and justice for my dad.

With tonight's recordings of Blackwood, this quest was made to order and called forth the best of my abilities. Izzy, I cannot just sit back and let this happen. I want to expose Blackwood and make sure people know the truth. But I am scared. I keep thinking about what happened to my dad, and I do not want to end up like him. But I cannot ignore this. I need your help. I know it's a lot to ask." I continued, my voice softer now. "But if we don't stand up to this, who will? I cannot let fear dictate my life. It's time to fight back."

Izzy's eyes widened, and there was a mix of distress and understanding. She leaned towards me, and after a deep breath, she finally responded, *"This journey might be as much for your dad as for those who have suffered in silence. From what you have told me, it is vital to stop their atrocious ideologies; their unstoppable greed and avarice must be revealed. It feels so dangerous; let me think about it."*

It was the perfect time to tell her I planned to take a copy of the recording to the FBI. I was surprised that she made an exception to my decision. I assured her it would bring this treasonous plot to the world.

Divulging my inadvertent spy craft is essential. With my emotions running deep, boldly, I replied, *"Even if it puts me in the line of fire, it is the right thing to do. I do not know where this conspiracy is going, but we cannot let them win. If we just let this go, then who will speak up and save democracy?"*

Izzy was taken aback and asked, "*Have you always been a caped crusader, like Superman leaping off tall buildings, protecting truth, justice, and the American way of life and fighting to expose the truth?*"

I smiled and began singing the celebrated song "*Superman's Got Nothing On Me!*"

Behind Closed Doors

*The only thing for the triumph of evil is
for good men to do nothing.*

~Edmund Burke

Chapter 18

Behind closed doors, where duplicity dwells, secrets whisper, and shadows dance, revealing the dark depths of deceit. We are being called to step up and stop the web of lies that attempt to entwine our fates.

I pulled out my phone with the Blackwood recording and asked, *"Izzy, let me reiterate: I do not want to jeopardize your career because you cannot unhear this. You are a trusted friend, and for tonight, you are not my boss, as I do not want to implicate you."*

She did not hesitate, *"Yes, Finn, there is much to consider. My concern is that this could lead us down a rabbit hole. Before you begin, I will close my office door."*

In a steady voice, I told her, *"Izzy, let me assure you, nothing could have prepared me to overhear Blackwood discussing shady business deals, the influence of foreign agencies, and an onslaught of toxic misinformation — propaganda unprecedented for the nation. Yet the real tragedy is that he is steering us toward autocracy."*

Her heart sank. Alarmed, Izzy said, *"Oh, Finn, we cannot allow history to repeat itself. This is an atrocity. We must do everything we can to prevent this happening. Our fight against tyranny will save the soul of humanity.*

I grew up listening to my mother and father recount their grandparents' horror stories of World War II's Hitler and Mussolini's regimes. Along with millions of others, they murdered my Italian and French great-grandparents. We will honor their legacy by standing up to Blackwood. Democracy, freedom, and human rights are worth fighting for. I am more than ready to listen to what you recorded."

I then tapped my phone's recording icon, and we heard…

JORDAN L. JAMES/SHARYN G. JORDAN

The Elephant
in the Room

When one with honeyed words but an evil mind
persuades the mob, great woes befall the state.

~Euripides

Chapter 19

The Senator cleared his throat and asked guests if they recalled the former Democratic President Lyndon Baines Johnson. Only one person was born when he was Commander in Chief, and that person was Blackwood. Nevertheless, in a ridiculous imitation of LBJ's Texas drawl, Blackwood boomed, "*My fellow Americans, I come to you with a heavy heart.*" Even though he meant it to be highly humorous, he bombed terribly.

Embarrassed but undaunted, Blackwood regrouped and began, "*As we know, your families gained immense wealth from the oil and gas industry. You will be grateful that our presidential nominee, Richard Ronald Tador, is beholding and wants to enrich your inheritance, which brings me here tonight.*

*As a homage to our oil-wealthy Lone Star state, allow me to try my Texas accent one more time and say that we have not been America as in the **G**rand **O**ld **P**arty for decades. Instead, we have long been the **G**as and **O**il **P**roject. On the first day of Tador's Presidency, he will dismantle the Environmental Protection Agency, EPA, which has held our GOP, as in the **G**as & **O**il **P**roject, hostage. Watch how we will drill, drill, drill. We will have more than enough government funds to create refineries as we free up natural parks for corporate use.*"

Only a select few will Blackwood disclose that behind him is a Cabal of superlobbyists and wealthy powers-that-be and are lurking behind closed doors.

He continued, "*Before the EPA laws were upgraded, we pulled the strings of environmental policies to serve our interests. When the previous administration successfully addressed what they believe is a real threat of climate change with an eye toward the future with its far-sighted initiatives to improve air quality, remove toxicities, and slow down the climate crisis, it became a burden on production. Government regulations have hamstrung us by regulating fracking and elevating air quality standards to reduce emissions. However, be assured: Our day has come!*

Influential figures whose vast fortunes and connections span industries, finance, and politics operate in the shadows. Through their secretive network of campaign contributions, Super PACs, and clandestine deals, these wealthy elites ensure that key decision-makers at the highest levels of government have already been swayed to remove strict environmental regulations set by the overzealous EPA and will reduce the high standards that stand in the way of profit margins. The catalyst is Tador."

Before the Senator could continue, Evelyn "Eve" Eden Everhart's authentic, charming Texas accent, abruptly interrupted him, saying, *"Excuse me, Senator, I believe what you want to convey is that our focus on fossil fuels will revitalize the economy and create jobs in struggling communities."*

I paused the recording at this critical cliffhanger moment, taking Izzy's arm, and suggested, *"Let's step outside and get some air."*

Standing under the starlit night, I said, *"Here we are, my friend, entangled in a political conflict that has taken me by storm. Even though our friendship in linear time is short, in other realms, it has been forever. Sharing laughter, food, and dreams has set a strong foundation for us to weather these tensions. You will be shocked at the toxicity of this world's poisonous bog!"*

Under the midnight sky, the air was cool and crisp; above us, the brilliant sky was illuminated by twinkling stars that seemed to pulse with life. This magical display starkly contrasted with the grim realities we faced and sparked something deep within us.

Izzy looked at the constellations, their formation reminding her of stories of heroes who had risen to challenges throughout history. We both felt a stir in our hearts, realizing we could be part of something bigger. She noted, *"If we don't step" up now, we might lose everything we care about."*

With her tears of gratitude streaming, she cried, *"All right. Let's do this."* She hugged me, and truth chills covered our entire beings. I nodded; her words inspired me: we knew the universe was urging us to act. With newfound clarity, we drew strength from the magic of the night. As we stood there, the stars resonated with our resolve, and once again, this time with my dear friend as my partner, a sense of purpose washed over both of us.

The possibility of a horrible outcome loomed, but we realized that fear could only thrive in silence. It is essential to ignite a spark of hope in the hearts of those around us. We knew the road would be difficult, but together, we would face it head-on, fueled by the belief that we could inspire change and protect the future. Determined, we stepped back inside, ready to continue listening.

Dearest Bridge Builder, The advantages of writing to you in the future are vast. For example, Eve is not who she appears to be.

SOMETHING ABOUT EVE

Climate change is real; it is happening right now. It is the most urgent threat facing our entire species, and we need to work collectively together to stop procrastinating.

~Leonardo Di Caprio

Chapter 20

Eve is a seasoned political strategist known for her sharp wit, no-nonsense approach, and ability to spin narratives and rally support, even for unpopular causes. Her complicated past, working for corporate interests and grassroots movements, gives her a unique perspective on these issues.

Hired by the Blackwood group and paid millions to act as his damage control person, she also knew a thing or two about boosting support for dismantling the EPA and furthering his aggressive oil plans.

Her father, James Jake Burnett, began his career as an Oil Wildcatter, a tried-and-tested rigger who worked his way up to being the CEO of International Obsidian Enterprises, a major player in this industry.

Indeed, Eve is not who they think she is. Her two-fold identity is more clearly defined: She presents a polished facade, embodying the confidence and charisma expected of a high-level consultant in the oil industry. She's a strong voice for this commerce. With sharp features framed by sleek, dark hair and piercing green eyes that seem to analyze everything around her, Eve is a master manipulator.

On the surface, she appears to be the perfect advocate for fossil fuel interests, pushing for deregulation and promising economic growth. As a prominent oil apostle, she is a persuasive activist; however, beneath a polished exterior lies a fierce determination driven by personal tragedy. Eve's father, who was bringing in green energy initiatives to complement fossil fuels, was mysteriously killed in a 'freak' oil derrick accident.

At first, the company ruled that negligent safety practices were to blame. When his loyal employees called foul play in a desperate move to protect the IOE's stock and reputation, her dad was portrayed as a corporate pension thief who had sabotaged the rig and somehow was killed in the process.

This injustice has fueled Eve's secret agenda: to gather evidence of the corruption that led to her father's death and expose Obsidian for what it truly is — greedy! She would beat them at their own game. She knows Blackwood is complicit since he is on the Board of Directors.

Eve dresses in exquisitely tailored suits that exude power, opting for the hues of indigo and black that mirror the depths of the ocean her father once worked in. Dressing for success is an affirmation of justice. All the while, she asks herself what he was even doing on a derrick in the ocean. At seventy-one years young, his recent knee replacement's grueling physical therapy sessions had sidelined him from most of his activities. Especially being on a derrick, which is known as a hazardous place due to fires, falls, and machinery failures. It did not make sense; she was determined to right this wrong.

Long before her dad suspiciously died, her career skyrocketed under the mentorship of a billionaire oil magnate, who recognized her as a rising star in both industries. She is involved in high-stakes negotiations and public relations campaigns designed to enhance Big Oil's image amidst growing environmental scrutiny.

Eve understands the intricacies of environmental regulations and how they impact the oil industry. She is well-versed in the historical ties between politics and petroleum. Eve knows which Senate committees hold the power to influence environmental legislation and has cultivated relationships with key players who can help her push the agenda. Her grasp of public sentiment is sharp; she knows how to frame arguments that resonate with her constituents and the broader public, emphasizing job creation and economic growth over environmental concerns.

Why should she care about what kind of world future generations will live in? Since she is unable to have children, a topic that is a significant trigger, her never-to-be-born grandchildren will not be poisoned by the toxic air that fossil fuels are creating.

Navigating the media landscape, Eve downplays the risks of dismantling the EPA. Her network of lobbyists and industry insiders allows her to gather intelligence on upcoming legislation and potential opposition. Through Blackwood, she has access to influential circles to leverage connections to fund campaigns that support her goals.

She is keenly aware of environmental science, enough to argue against it effectively without appearing ignorant. She uses this knowledge strategically, often citing studies that soften the impact of oil drilling on climate change while dismissing opposing views as overly alarmist.

Eve is playing a long game, skillfully maneuvering within the circles of power. She uses her position to gain intel on corporate practices, building a network of allies who share her vision for reform. As she navigates the treacherous waters of corporate politics, she carefully cultivates a dual identity: the loyal employee promoting big oil and an undercover whistleblower seeking justice. Her intelligence and resourcefulness make her a formidable adversary, capable of turning the tables on those who believe they are untouchable.

Throughout her journey, unlike Jax, Eve does not wrestle with the ethical implications of her actions, torn between the wealth and influence she has gained and the moral imperative to seek justice for her father. She is relentless, driven by vengeance that fuels her every move, and as she draws closer to unveiling the truth, she risks everything — her career, her freedom, and her life. In a world where trust is scarce and betrayal is commonplace, it is a force to be reckoned with; she is determined to flip the script and hold the powerful accountable for their sins.

Her charisma allows her to win over skeptics, making her a formidable advocate for the corrupt Senator's agenda. She manipulates public opinion by outlining environmental regulations as government overreach, appealing to a sense of individualism and freedom that resonates with many people. In private meetings, she discusses strategy with the Senator, sharing insights on weakening the EPA's authority through legislative loopholes and budget cuts. She knows the importance of timing and patience and has waited years to strike when the political iron or climate is right.

Izzy's expression was as if she had seen a ghost. She whispered in a rather eerie tone, "*Finn, as you know, I receive intuitive images that I call "conversations with" or "downloads from the universe."* With all you have told me about your grandmother's sixth sense, you will understand this skill and believe in my instinctual gifts.

Izzy was intrigued about Eve and had a hunch that even though her plight was ruthless, she might be our ally. Then, true to her intuitive gifts, she envisioned a mystery man, a multi-billionaire who craves power. Like Napolean Bonapart, Genghis Khan, and Alexander the Great, all megalomaniacs, he is the puppet master; I will call him Emperor. He has an even darker energy than Blackwood or Tador. I concur with Izzy. Someone is pulling the GOP's strings and making them dance to his tune. Why not Emperor?

Indeed, the plot thickens; the Emperor will come into play. Unbeknownst to Blackwood and especially Tador, this maniacal saboteur is a megalomaniac who has his interest. He is a Ninja behind the scenes who has secretly been hiding in plain sight yet has worked for years to influence our political landscape. With billions in his court, his diabolical scheme will tear apart the very fabric of our democracy. He is the ultimate autocrat.

We knew plots, plans, and programs were getting more interesting. This uncanny political story unfolded rapidly and kept our curiosity stimulated.

The Great Reveal

Everything you have seen here is an illusion.

~Edward Norton

Chapter 21

Resuming the tell-tale recording reveals the distinctive voice of Alex Longwell, who said, "**Blackwood, you are on a fool's errand!** We want **nothing** to do with your proposal; we are not furthering your agenda."

Your nominee, Richard "Dick" Ronald Tador, as in Dick-Tay-Dor, is not qualified to be the Commander in Chief. History reminds us that there have already been two corrupt Dicks in the White House, both of whom were GOP'ers."

Audacious humor found a firm footing, and the room erupted with laughter. Just the mention of Dick Tador's name, pronounced as DICTATOR, was hysterical. He played on the evil moniker's inferences as an entertainer and podcaster. The guests howled, yet Alex's truths were not diminished.

Alex reminded the group that the thinly veiled attempt to make Tador another Ross Perot, who ran for president in 1992 as an independent candidate, was misguided. Perot was a successful, honest businessman who wanted to focus on balancing the federal budget, reducing the national debt, and effectively reforming government. Tador does not have this type of business acumen, diplomacy, or skill set; he is a fraud.

With a curious look on her face, once again, Izzy paused the recording. Being unfamiliar with American Politics, she asked who these Dicks were.

Finn answered, *"For the record, President Richard Millhouse, 'Tricky Dick' Nixon of the notorious scandal called Watergate. He resigned right before he was sure to be impeached and was the first president ever to do so.*

Another one is the most reviled politician in history, the orchestrator of the Haliburton Oil Company Fiasco, and, yes, the very man who intentionally sent our service people to Iraq to murder and to be murdered, VP Dick Cheney. Of course, there have long been conspiracy theories and speculation about his ulterior motives behind the United States' decision to invade Iraq. Many critics suggested that Cheney had a vested interest in the region's oil reserves and that the invasion was driven by a desire to secure access to Iraq's substantial petroleum wealth.

These claims fueled accusations that the Iraq War was, at least in part, motivated by economic interests rather than the stated reasons for combating terrorism or eliminating weapons of mass destruction. The latter proved to be non-existent. Izzy, the only weapon of Mass Destruction, is Dick Tador, who wants to be the Dictator.

Big oil influencing political decisions has long been an ongoing situation. Izzy, wait until you hear more about these recorded exchanges."

Given what you had said about the Mystery Man, I knew only too well how surreal this must be for you. Empathetically, I asked, "What do you think so far?"

She looked at me in utter disbelief, stood up, and stated, "I would have never imagined it if I had not heard with my ears. My God, it seems like science fiction. It is revolting."

I nodded in agreement and clicked the recording back alive; Alex was still speaking. "From the heart of Pennsylvania, I am beyond blessed to be part of a wealthy oil family with deep roots in the region's energy sector. I have always taken a respectful responsibility for having inherited a vast fortune built on decades of oil drilling and production.

Similarly, Amalie came from a lineage of successful Oklahoma oil magnates who had long dominated the market. However, we both share a vision that transcends our family's legacy. We recognized the urgent need for sustainable practices and embarked on a transformational journey. Once staunch advocates for traditional energy sources, each of our grandparents had come to understand that the world was changing. They embraced the idea that oil had served its profound purpose and would always have a place in our world. Yet, let us reduce our carbon footprint and its negative impact on breathing in clean air. Creating a sustainable future is paramount for future generations.

With this newfound perspective, we established the Longwell Foundation for Renewable Innovation, which is dedicated to funding research and development in green energy technologies. Our entire family believes investing in sustainable sources is an ethical imperative and a *smart financial move for the future. Our foundation has already funded several forward-thinking projects, including solar farms and wind turbine installations, helping to create jobs and stimulate local economies in Pennsylvania, Oklahoma, and other oil-rich states.*

Meanwhile, we are diligently raising awareness about the importance of transitioning to renewable energy and supporting communities in making that switch. We have partnered with schools and local governments to provide educational resources and infrastructure improvements to reduce carbon foot-prints and promote environmental stewardship.

We are grateful philanthropists and passionate advocates for progressive policy change. We frequently engage with lawmakers to promote legislation that supports renewable energy incentives and infrastructure development. Our efforts have garnered attention, inspiring other families in the energy sector to consider their wealth's impact and contribute to a cleaner, more viable world. Through our philanthropic foundations, we are forging a path that honors our family's legacy while bravely stepping into a new era of responsibility.

We believe that true wealth lies in the ability to effect positive change, ensuring that clean air and a thriving planet are lasting gifts we can pass on to future generations. Our collaborative efforts testify to the power of transformation and hope, proving that even the most entrenched industries can evolve.

Blackwood, you are out of step with the times. This is not the direction we see our nation going. We will not go along with your diabolical plot to undermine our grandchildren's future. And now, please excuse us as we are taking our leave."

Finn paused the recording after seeing Izzy's tears streaming down her flushed cheeks. Alex's bold declaration brought dignity, truth, and courage into a treacherous Blackwood environment.

Without one word, Izzy and I exchanged compassionate looks. She had fully grasped the immensity of Senator Blackwood's unnerving plans. We drank our herbal tea silently and breathed deeply to collect our thoughts. I reminded Izzy that Theo, Maggie, and the Wycliffs also remained in the room. Blackwood was a malicious Houdini trying to pull the wool over everyone's eyes.

The Wycliffs

*Continuous effort, not strength or intelligence,
is the key to unlocking our potential.*

~Winston Churchill

Chapter 22

The wise and composed William 'Will' Winston Wycliff, Esquire, a shrewd business tycoon known for his generosity, sat cradling the hands of his wife, Charlotte Hawthorn Wycliff, best-selling author. I observed the Senator slowly sipping his now-cold coffee and, with steely eyes, glaring directly at the tycoon and his wife.

Although I did not record it, I overheard Will whispering to Charlotte, *"Darling, you must be as befuddled as I am. It is a curious situation, so let us not condone or condemn anything Blackwood proposes. First, we will listen without interruption."*

Once the recording resumes, we hear Blackwood asking Eve to take the spotlight with a rebuttal. She is surprised yet always prepared and politely addresses the two remaining couples.

Eve begins with a politico statement worthy of her reputation for being an expert on Spin, *"Crafting a narrative to support Dick Tador, an unqualified politician, took some deep diving. As a strategist, I decided to emphasize a message centered around efficiency and effectiveness. I made a compelling argument that downsizing government is essential for streamlining operations and reducing waste, suggesting that a leaner government can lead to more responsive and responsible governance.*

Focusing on the idea that less bureaucracy allows for more significant individual freedom positions this inexperienced politician as a champion of personal liberties. As a strategist, I pointed out to Tador that highlighting the benefits of local governance, asserting that decisions made closer to the people are more representative of their needs. This could create an appeal to those who feel disconnected from federal politics, portraying the politician as a unifier who prioritizes community values over inaccessible political agendas.

Furthermore, Blackwood, Tador, and I are framing the narrative around economic growth, arguing that a smaller government will foster a more vibrant economy by reducing clean air regulations that stifle innovation and entrepreneurship. This approach could resonate with business owners and those who believe in free-market principles. In addition, we are tapping into the sentiment of a populist movement, claiming that this politician listens to the concerns of everyday Americans and aims to empower them.

By presenting the government curtailment of its inflated bureaucracy as a necessary step toward revitalizing American democracy, we will create a compelling argument for why this politician is the right choice for the future. Ultimately, the goal is to present a vision where downsizing is seen not as a threat but as a transformative opportunity, positioning Tador as a necessary leader for a new era of American governance.

At another time, we will discuss women's health care, or as Walter Cronkite once said, "America's health care system is neither healthy nor caring nor a system." *The topics of immigration, abortion, and the horrifically heartbreaking drug fentanyl will be a significant issue. We are staying away from Tador's history.*

Will takes a minute and looks directly at Blackwood, Jax, the Kensington's, and Eve. He thanks her for her clever strategy of making someone so shallow as DICTADOR look somewhat worthy of running for the highest office in our nation.

To a vast many people, Dick is charismatic; however, every unpleasant, unethical, and unbelievable action you have heard about him is correct. He has lived a privileged, hedonistic, and, yes, superficial life and is far removed from the everyday person's challenges. He has cheated, lied, and been unfaithful to wives, workers, and wannabes. He is known for his boardroom and backroom deals.

For years, Tador has pretended to be wealthy, yet this campaign platform afforded him a robust merchandise boutique that bailed him out of extreme financial woes. That isn't something we have ever seen and probably never will again. Something else we will never see is an apology, not restitution, to my wife Charlotte's brother, whom Tador not only ruined financially but mentally and emotionally.

There is a psychological edge to his harsh rhetoric that will attract voters who are fed up with their own lives. They will resonate with his immature and cruel bullying and blaming of the government with a shared rage.

With only Theo, Maggie, Eve, and Jax left in the spacious dining room, Blackwood stands and shares, "I am proud to say we have orchestrated an elaborately lucrative campaign, pouring money into Dick, ensuring he has all the resources he needs. We have carefully crafted his image, guiding his speeches and public appearances, making him a vessel for our agenda.

As the campaign progresses, we feel confident that we will continue pulling his strings at will, steering Dick in the direction that suits our interests. Let's face it: Dick Tador is motivated to serve on our terms.

As per the commander-in-chief, he understands the value of being the CEO of America, and we, the board of directors, who have long known our strengths, are guiding him. What could go wrong?"

CONFRONTATION

The only way to deal with fear is to face it head on.

~Tony Robbins

CHAPTER 23

Once again, I pause the recording and ask Izzy, "*I know this is shocking. What do you think so far?*"

Her expression is sheer horror; she nods yes and says, "*It is unbelievable that Blackwood thinks he could get away with this treasonous plot. Every word he has said is a dagger aimed at the heart of the people. This is not just corruption; it's a betrayal on a scale I never imagined. Finn, you must get this information out, but please be careful. If they find out you have these recordings, you will put your writing and composing career on the line and your life in danger. But we can't let them destroy everything my ancestors lost their lives and fought for. The truth must come out, no matter what the cost.*"

Resuming where we left off on the recording, we could hear Will's solemn voice ardently utter, "*Senator, mark my words; you are on the wrong side of history! How can you believe that my wife Charlotte, whose books and lifelong work have long stood for progress, and I, an innovator and influencer, would ever agree to support such an outlandish plan? Your plot will ultimately set back the tremendous efforts already in motion to successfully curtail climate change.*

Have you no conscience? Because of fossil fuels, we know that apocalyptic fires are burning up our towns, canyons, and forests; toxic waters carry poisons, and community voices are crying out for peace, balance, and a return to harmony. The chaos can feel overwhelming — like a tidal wave pulling us under. The oceans are warming, and hurricanes are becoming more frequent. Their rapid storms are growing into massive, sprawling monsters whose intensifying strength leads to higher than ever recorded wind speeds and rising sea levels. One of the factors is fossil fuels.

Tador believes Climate Change is a hoax, and right before our eyes, we see its altering weather patterns creating severe droughts, rampant wildfires, and heavy rainfall events. These natural disasters exacerbate flash floods, tornadoes, and landslides like never before. How can you not agree with the importance of taking action to reduce greenhouse gas emissions?

A misguided plot like yours will negatively change the course of our future, a plan that could lead to... well, you get the picture, the destruction of humanity as we know it. And for what, money, power, and greed?

Blackwood, I challenge you to tell your grandchildren about your maniacal plans to rob them of their future. Let them know you are stealing their clean air, creating a world that will choke them to death, flood, and ruin their cherished earth, and will initiate havoc like no other generations before them will have ever seen.

There are far too many conservatives who would love to see the resurrection of our Creator and bring in the rapture. It is important to note that God is Love, not war! For centuries, His name has been used in vain to massacre the innocent, justify ethnic cleansing, instigate genocide, the Holocaust, and the four Inquisitions of the Medieval, Spanish, Portuguese, and Roman; these are only a few of the inhuman atrocities. Charlotte and I believe Christ's Consciousness came into this world and in our hearts and brought peace, love, and harmony. You are ushering in a gratuitous Armageddon; how do you sleep at night, you pompous bastard?"

Hand in hand, in disgust yet in dignity, Charlotte and Will depart. They notice that I am standing behind the theatre-length drapes, out of Senator Blackwood's eyesight, and recognize I am recording the diabolical scheme. Will gives me a thumb-up, and Charlotte pantomimes for me to call them. Bidding farewell, the Country Club stood silent. Its majestic walls held the dark secrets of the evening within.

The Crafty Kensington

Not all snakes slither. Some walk among us.

~Unknown

Chapter 24

Before Finn restarts the recording, he notes that Blackwood has turned all his attention toward Theodore 'Theo' Benjamin and Maggie Kensington; this begs the question, who among the eight powerful couples will be tempted by the snake and sell their soul to the devil?

This was the perfect opportunity to ask Izzy what, if anything, she knew about Mr. and Mrs. Kensington: he, a controversial media mogul thirsty for power, and her, a superficial, shallow socialite whose family is rumored to have long-standing connections to the underworld?

After carefully considering it, she replied, "*Only the juicy gossip circulating among the staff. They never tip more than a pittance, argue over trivial things with our servers, and always stir up some ridiculously unfounded complaint. That alone is enough to make you disrespect them.*"

I filled her in on Theo's dubious yet meteoric rise to success, which began immediately after he became engaged to Maggie. Since she was accustomed to a particularly elite lifestyle, with the help of her influential father, Magnus Markham Mayfield, Theo's acquisition of the WFTP Radio and Television station served both interests. They were the perfect opportunists.

Clicking my phone's recording icon into the play mode, we could hear Blackwood speaking with this last couple. With the full attention of this wealthy, superpower couple, the Senator was confident he could lay out his entire devious plan.

Senator Blackwood resumed, "*It is with great pleasure that you are open to benefiting far beyond your wildest expectations. Our future President, Richard Ronald Tador, will deeply appreciate your support and reciprocate and reward you accordingly.*

Even though Genesis Wentworth Wordsmith is currently polling far ahead of Dick, regardless of the popular vote, we have the Electoral College wrapped up, and the fix is in."

Instead of being appalled, Theo and Maggie were even more enthralled. In unison, they gleefully asked, "How will we be compensated, specifically?"

Blackwood replied, "*There are a myriad ways Dick can show his appreciation. For example, Theo, you own a Radio and Television Media Conglomerate, WFTP. Think of the advertising angles, the social media spikes, hikes, and likes. Of course, the opportunity to be a controversial edge stirs up anger. We know this persuasion always brings out the disenfranchised.*

As Dick's favorite go-to network, you will create a captivating platform for those people who have been marginalized, misguided, and who are mad at the government, blaming the Progressives for not having achieved the life they thought they deserved.

It is much easier to believe anything and everything negative. This contentious discourse will gain millions of new audiences and help us dismantle the policies that prevent us from making profits.

And for you, Maggie, Dick is quite the charmer. Think of how envious your social circle will be of your close friendship with the next President of the United States. You will receive unlimited VIP invitations to your choice of White House dinners. Plus, hobknobbing with the global elite is a dynamic, notable change for both of you. If you think your circle is influential now, wait until you are in the place of the chosen."

I reminded Izzy that Blackwood is a seasoned smooth talker who was pleased to optimize this luxury location to lure Theo and Maggie into his corrupt plans. His pitch perfectly matched their desires for additional privilege and indulgence, promising access to power and influence offered only in such prestigious surroundings. If he succeeded, the Senator would gain billions of dollars for his GOP and private investments.

Hungrily, Maggie and Theo exchanged glances that sent me the creepiest shivers. The married couple, notorious for their manipulative ways and relentless pursuit of power and status at the expense of others, had earned them a reputation as ruthless and unscrupulous individuals.

Due to their questionable morals and deceitful tactics, they were open to furthering their interests, even if it meant harming those around them. Their actions were a stark reminder of the darker side of human nature, in the throes of greed and ambition.

Blackwood assured them, *"Dick is easily swayed with favors and flattery. You will see his desperation to be in power. Remember, these very same character "flaws" is precisely how we appealed to him.*

With his worship of being adored, he drank in every admiration we poured into him. But beneath this facade lies a secret: a mission to uncover potentially damaging information that he possesses about every senator. As one of his several puppet masters, I assure you he will prove incredibly valuable in letting us write our long-term policies. Dick Tador is the quintessential court jester and cannot help himself from behaving irreverently. This is only the tip of the iceberg…"

We paused the recording, and Izzy referred to Blackwood's 'iceberg' comment, suggesting that additional disinformation, dismantling, and disruptions would be revealed. She is spot on; this gets darker.

"It is shocking to hear these sinister plans. Oh, Finn, the news of election interference, foreign falsities, and play-to-pay politics exists in echo chambers of such horrific ideologies. Let us believe significant advances are now happening, and trust will be restored. So much evolution is occurring at warp speed.

Ironically, Artificial Intelligence will eventually provide government transparency. This disclosure shocks those who seek to use it in malevolent ways. Positive shifts are coming for humanity! The Universe has blessed us to know nothing is as it seems. It is up to us to create peace in the world, our homes, and our hearts. The scale of our paths is vast, the speed is exponential, and the scope of our work is spiritual.

Please, Finn, tell me Genesis is forward-moving, works for the people, cares about humanity, and understands the rule of law."

I said, *"I can promise she is. Let me tell you about her."*

The Promise

The hand that rocks the cradle rules the world.

~H.W. Beecher

Chapter 25

Enter Genesis Wren Wentworth Wordsworth is possibly the first woman president and will not be the last. As a Progressive Presidential Nominee, she is a highly respected public servant and seasoned politician; she is overwhelmingly respected.

She is the first to know that a person cannot please everyone. They are answerable to themselves, and if they are social justice warriors, which she is, they are bound by their moral code to fulfill their responsibility of creating a better world.

Born in Washington, DC, on November 18, 1953, in the first year of what would be her father's two-term, highly celebrated, and influential Presidency, Genesis's upbringing in a close-knit family included two older brothers. Yet, tragically, her twin sister, Gillian "Gilly" Wonderment Wordsmith, was stillborn.

In her recent Memoir, she shared, "The joy of my birth was overshadowed by the sorrow of Gilly's passing, a grief that would haunt my mother and inspire me throughout our lives.

This loss shaped her understanding of life's fragility. It was an honor and a responsibility to also live for her sister. Gilly's passing instilled a remarkable resilience that is a testament to the human spirit's ability to overcome adversity. Growing up, Genesis observed the value of education and civic engagement. Her dad, the Commander in Chief, instilled in her a strong sense of social justice and modeled the importance of giving back to her community. She is a visionary leader dedicated to serving others and improving the world. Genesis's journey toward becoming a presidential candidate began long before she dreamed of holding such a prestigious office.

From a young age, she was driven by a deep compassion and a burning desire to create positive change in the world. This drive led her to pursue a career in public service, where she worked tirelessly to uplift communities, empower marginalized groups, and fight for social justice.

Her brave body of work was a testament to her commitment to making a difference. Her diverse experiences molded her into the formidable leader she is today.

As she embarked on her journey to the presidency, Genesis's lifetime of service became a central pillar of her campaign. There was no doubt she could lead the country towards a brighter future. Genesis's supporters pointed to her track record of success in tackling some of the most pressing issues of our time. She has spearheaded initiatives to combat poverty, promote education, and protect the environment.

Her ability to bring people together, regardless of their background or beliefs, earned her a reputation as a unifier and a bridge builder. However, what sets Genesis apart is her sincerity, which resonates with people from all walks of life and draws them to her message of hope and progress.

As Genesis stood on the debate stage, facing off against her opponents, her presence was commanding yet approachable. She spoke eloquently and passionately, outlining her bold vision for a more just and equitable society. Although her opponents may have had their talking points and political strategies, Genesis's authenticity, depth of experience, and vision showed she was the best candidate for the job. In the days leading up to the election, Genesis crisscrossed the country, meeting with voters, listening to their concerns, and addressing their hopes for the future.

She engaged in town hall meetings, visited schools and community centers, and participated in grassroots events to connect with people on a personal level. Her supporters saw in her a beacon of hope, a symbol of a brighter tomorrow where everyone had a chance to thrive and succeed. They believed in her ability to lead with integrity, compassion, and a deep sense of purpose.

As the election day drew nearer, the excitement and anticipation reached a fevered pitch. Young and old, rich and poor, came out in droves to support Genesis "Gen" Wentworth. They believed in her vision for a better future where everyone has access to quality healthcare, education, and opportunities for success. Time is shifting into its proper place of freedom, expressed artistry, and humanity's joy from centuries of suppression, inequality, and bias into strong, safe, and sacred systems.

Knowing Genesis was the leader who could move our country forward, my recording of Blackwood's devious plots and duplicitous plans to dismantle democracy and our future, which I now call Oak-Gate, was essential to reveal.

It's All Greek

*I guess darkness serves a purpose to show us
that there is redemption through chaos.
I believe that is the basis for Greek Mythology.*

~Brendan Fraser

Chapter 26

"*Finn, let us take a break from this intense situation. To help us lighten up, it is perfect timing to read you a letter from my childhood friend Marisol, who wrote me about her brilliant turn of luck...*"

My Dearest Izzy,

I trust this letter of gratitude finds you well. I am amazed it has been three years since we last enjoyed our Celebration Cuppas in person. With the Eiffel Tower glistening behind us, we were in Paris, overlooking the Seine River under the night sky's canopy of stars. I had just completed my doctorate in Greek Mythology — please call me Dr. Mirasol Zara — and simultaneously, you were enroute to your dream job in America.

I am thrilled to share the Great Good News, and I will see you sooner rather than later. During these past three months, my original MUSE-ical, the **Vale of Inspiration, sold out in all its venues.** Our tour took us to Baltic Europe, France, Italy, and Ireland — oh, it has been just a time of divine alchemy.

Drum Roll, Please. I just signed a lucrative contract to bring it to Broadway! As you can imagine, I am ecstatic! Of course, it came about in part because you believed in me. I am deeply grateful for your encouragement.

You may wonder how I received such an incredible offer. On her fourth time attending our performance, the foremost Broadway producer, Matilda Marjorie McIntyre, asked to meet me. It was divine synchronicity; yes, it was fate. Indeed, luck always favors the prepared.

Matilda said that besides being enthralled by the musical's timely, far-reaching message, she was fascinated by my spot-on face-reading analysis. It will not surprise you to know that I continue to engage with our audiences by sharing my Romani - Gypsy roots of the blessings of Face Reading. I continue to delight in translating precisely what the faces of those interested are saying.

Last night, I was asked about the face of the entertainer turned politician Dick Tador. I was intrigued when I saw a photo of him and Senator Blackwood standing by his side.

This is a heads-up to your American friends and the world: both men have eyes of what is called 'Dead Wood,' which means they have challenged livers and are angry. These features indicate significant issues related to stagnation, lack of growth, or difficulty moving forward. This compromised organ sets up a pattern of power-mongering and blaming others for their lack of joy. Be extremely wary of them.

And, back to my brilliant news, a segment of my musical delves into the age-old purgatory of pastors and priests using their pulpits to preach petty politics to their parishioners. We know this has happened repeatedly in history. Yet, through our arts, we are bringing in a future of lasting peace. We are at a tipping point when empathy, wisdom, and humanity 'Stand Together as our Birth 'Writes.'

My dearest friend, I am honored to include your and Finn's tickets for my Broadway Opening. I love you.

As always,
Marisol

P.S. I have included a bare-bones script. I know imagination will fill in the blanks.

The Muse

Myths are archetypal patterns in human consciousness.

~Joseph Campbell

CHAPTER 27

My darling Izzy,

1 t is a delight to share the original draft of my MUSE-ical with you. Pour yourself one of your delicious cuppa teas and drink in its goodness. To not spoil your Broadway experience of a visually stunning production, to tell a tale that has been told from time immortal in a fairy tale version is divine. This reminds us that our creative self is only an 'ask away" and dwells within at the Vale of Inspiration.

In Greek, Latin, French, and English, the word muse's derivative is a place of study, library, shrine, temple, museum, and mosaic. Oh, Izzy, you and I adore the mystery, miracles, magic, and mystical essences of the Mythos, which means the word, story, and speech. As we know, a Myth bridges the unknown to the known and connects humanity to the mystery.

Our myths inform and shape what already exists within us, the ineffable essence of our story of origin. Its language is encoded within our eternal selves. We are weaving our tapestry of love with the threads of nature's finest artistry; we are blessed.

When people become so severe that they do not hear their muse, their creativity is stifled, and they grow listless. With whimsy, wonder, and wisdom, my MUSE-ical speaks of the end of an era and our welcoming in a new time of tremendous change. Interestingly, these brilliant insights are revealed by the ancient Nine Muses. Their archetypal energies give us the strength, power, and ability to restart, renew, and refine our intentions, dreams, and wishes. Their opulently operative words are sustainability, luminosity, and reciprocity.

The Vale resides within our inner realms, where emerald streams course through our blood and bones. It is a domain of enchanting beauty that unfolds like a dream. The waterways flow gracefully, reflecting the sky's hues and the lush surroundings, creating a serene atmosphere that invites exploration and contemplation. Gentle streams meander, their crystalline waters whispering secrets as they dance over smooth stones and weave through vibrant patches of wildflowers. Surrounding these waterways are magical forests, where towering trees stretch their limbs high into the heavens, their leaves shimmering with an ethereal glow.

Sunlight filters through the leafy canopy, illuminating the rich tapestry of life that flourishes below moss that carpets the earth like lush velvet, while delicate ferns sway gently in the dappled light, their fronds unfurling in graceful arcs. Here, the air is thick with the earthy scent of soil, mingling with the sweet perfume of blooming wildflowers, each hue a brilliant stroke on nature's canvas. while the gentle rustle of leaves tells a timeless tale of the wind's playful journey.

In this sphere, every corner reveals exquisitely vibrant colors of the thousands of blossoms. Animals move gracefully through the underbrush, their presence adding to the sense of harmony and balance. The songs of birds fill the air, their melodies harmonizing with the gentle sounds of the flowing water, creating a symphony of bliss that resonates deep within the soul. A sense of peace envelops the spirit as one wanders through the Vale of Inspiration.

The combination of picturesque landscapes, the soothing presence of water, and the enchanting forests fosters an environment where creativity flourishes and inspiration flows freely. It is a sanctuary where the heart finds solace, and the mind can wander to realms of imagination and dreams. In this magical place, beauty and bliss intertwine, offering a glimpse into a world where nature reigns supreme and every moment feels like a bejeweled and precious gift.

This is a sanctuary for the Nine Muses, divine daughters of Zeus and Mnemosyne, each embodying a different aspect of the arts and sciences. Clio, the Muse of history, guided the threads of the past; Calliope, the Muse of epic poetry, inspired grand tales of heroism; and so on through the enchanting ensemble: Erato for love poetry, Euterpe for music, Melpomene for tragedy, Polyhymnia for sacred hymns, Terpsichore for dance, Thalia for comedy, and Urania for astronomy.

The Muses live in harmony, each nurturing their respective gifts while drawing inspiration from one another. They would often gather around the crystal-clear waters of a luminous lake, where the reflections of the mountains created a tapestry of colors that ignited their creativity. However, as time passed, they began to sense a growing discontent in the world beyond their value. All the Artists struggled to find their voices, and scholars grappled with the weight.

One day, Calliope, moved by humanity's plight, proposed a bold idea: *"Let us descend from our vale and share our gifts with the world. It is time for us to inspire those who seek to create and cultivate."* The other Muses, intrigued yet hesitant, deliberated.

Clio reminded her elegant sisters of the importance of writing, primarily chronicling history, but Melpomene feared the pain of the human experience might overwhelm them. However, the spark of inspiration burned brightly in their hearts, and they ultimately agreed to help.

The Muses set forth, cloaked in shimmering light, their presence filling the air with an ethereal melody. As they reached the outskirts of the valley, they found the village where artists and thinkers struggled with despair. They witnessed a painter staring at a blank canvas, a poet lost for words, and a musician with a broken instrument. The Muses, filled with compassion, decided to intervene.

Euterpe approached the musician first, her fingers dancing through the air as she conjured a gentle breeze. The wind wrapped around the musician, carrying a symphony of sounds — birds chirping, leaves rustling, and children's laughter. Inspired by this, the musician picked up his instrument, and melodies flowed from him like a river, filling the village with music.

Meanwhile, Calliope found the poet, whose heart was heavy with unspoken words. She whispered of ancient heroes and their noble deeds into his ear, weaving stories of love and sacrifice. The poet's eyes widened as images of valor and beauty danced in his mind. With newfound passion, he seized his quill and began to write verses flowing like a waterfall.

As the sun dipped low in the sky, casting golden rays upon the village, Terpsichore approached the painter, who had long given up hope. With a graceful twirl, she beckoned him to dance. Hesitant at first, he soon found himself swept away by her energy, his feet moving to a rhythm only he could hear. The movement stirred something deep within him, and he felt a rush of colors and emotions welling up. He dashed back to his canvas, and with every stroke of his brush, he painted not just a picture but a vivid expression of his soul.

In the corners of the village, the other Muses worked their magic. Melpomene inspired the townsfolk to confront their sorrows, transforming despair into poignant tales of resilience. Clio shared stories of the past, reminding the villagers of their heritage and the strength that came from their ancestors. Polyhymnia led the community in songs of gratitude and reverence, uniting them in a chorus that resonated through the valley. As night fell, the villagers gathered around a flickering fire, the air sliced with creativity and camaraderie. They shared their new-found works of wondrously inspired music, poetry, and dance, their hearts swelling at the sight of inspiration igniting within the hearts of mortals.

But the Muses also realized that their presence was more than just a fleeting moment of magic. It was a reminder that creativity and knowledge were not gifts to be hoarded but shared, nurtured, and celebrated. They decided to stay a while longer, teaching the villagers the importance of inspiration, collaboration, and the strength found in the community. Days turned into weeks, and the village flourished. Artists and thinkers continued to emerge, each uniquely inspired by the Muses. They learned to draw from one another, collaborate, and innovate

The Vale of Inspiration was no longer just a hidden sanctuary; it was alive and well within each person; it had become a beacon of hope for all who sought creativity. With a gentle breeze, they promised to watch over the village constantly. Before they left, Calliope addressed the villagers gathered around the lake. "Remember, dear friends, that inspiration is like a flame. It can flicker and fade but can be reignited with love, passion, and community. Share your gifts and watch as they multiply."

The villagers' souls overflowed with gratitude. They promised to uphold the spirit of creativity and to honor the Muses in their works. The Muses resumed their tranquil existence in the Vale of Inspiration, yet their hearts were forever changed. They spent their days weaving new tales of human creativity and emotions, drawing inspiration from the vibrant village they had once visited. The stories of the villagers became part of their eternal tapestry, enriching the fabric of art and knowledge for generations to come. In time, the villagers became known far and wide for their extraordinary talents.

The villagers established a festival in honor of the Muses, celebrating art, music, poetry, and knowledge that drew people from distant lands. Artists, poets, musicians, and scholars gathered to share their works and learn from one another, creating and cultivating a vibrant community that flourished in collaboration.

Annually, they gather by the lake, lighting lanterns that float into the sky like twinkling stars. They tell stories of their struggles and triumphs, sing songs of love and loss, and dance under the moonlight, honoring the Muses who had sparked their creativity. On the inner planes of existence, the bond between the majestic Muses and the villagers grew stronger, transcending the boundaries of the divine and the mortal. The Muses would occasionally make their presence known, offering symbols of encouragement, and the villagers would feel the warmth of their inspiration in every brushstroke, lyric, and note. The Vale of Inspiration became a place of pilgrimage for those seeking the Muses' blessing.

And so, the legacy of the Nine Muses lived on not just in storytelling but in the hearts of every artist and scholar who dared to dream. Their essence infused the beauty of creativity, the bliss of imagination, and the blessings of inspiration. A connection to something greater than themselves.

All this good news sent Izzy's heart swirling. With an optimistic smile, she refreshed our tea, turned off the music, and moved her comfortable chair closer to mine. She was ready to feed her appetite, a growing intrigue, and dive deeper into my mysterious narrative revealing that corrupt politicians are burning down long-standing democratic processes. Izzy knew this mission would take us into a dark web of deceit however she trusted me.

Her curiosity was peeked when I told her we are not only Bridge Builders we are called to be the Phoenix. This mythical bird bursts into flames and is consumed by fire, only to rise again from its ashes, emerging reborn and revitalized. This cycle of death and rebirth represents the idea of overcoming challenges, the potential for new beginnings, and the resilience of life. As Phoenix, we embody and embrace the enduring nature of the spirit, signifying courage and the ability to rise above adversity.

In a nation on the brink of authoritarianism, finding ourselves at the forefront of a battle for democracy, I would not let the sacrifices of past generations be forgotten. Fueled by a deep-seated belief in freedom, justice, and the rule of law, witnessing intimidation, misinformation, and the plans to gut federal, civil, environmental, and intelligence agencies is heartbreaking. Senator Blackwood's tragic betrayal was in the league with dangerous ideologues.

Ultimately, I pray we weave a story that strengthens the fragility of democracy, the power of collective action, and our enduring spirit that refuses to stand idly by as our freedoms are not only threatened, they are being dismantled. We are reminded that the fight for democracy is ongoing and that each of us has a role in shaping the future. God bless America.

AN OILY PROPOSITION

Fire made us human; fossil fuels made us modern,
but now we need a new fire that makes us safe,
secure, healthy, and durable.

~Amory Lovins

Chapter 28

S till sorting who is who and why is why, Izzy wanted to know more about Blackwood's Gas and Oil Project statement. As a history buff, I gave her an excellent overview:

"When *the clouds of Civil War darkened the horizon, and the nation stood on the brink of conflict, a Republican Party, the Grand Old Party, the GOP, was born — a beacon of light in a time of darkness, a symbol of courage and resilience in the face of great adversity.*

Led by Abraham Lincoln and Horace Greeley, Republicans laid the foundation for a new era of American history, one defined by the triumph of liberty over oppression and the enduring legacy of a nation united in its pursuit of justice.

Beginning in 1854, the United States was in the throes of a heated debate over the expansion of slavery into the newly acquired territories. When the specter of civil war loomed on the horizon, the political landscape seemed ill-equipped to address the day's pressing issues. The new party was needed to champion the cause of liberty and equality for all.

The newly founded Republican Party embarked on a mission to challenge the status quo and reshape the nation's future. Party members traveled far and wide, delivering impassioned speeches, rallying support, and inspiring others to join their cause. Despite opposition from entrenched political interests and powerful adversaries, the GOP stood firm in its convictions and refused to back down. They knew the road ahead would be long and arduous, but they were willing to make whatever sacrifices necessary to achieve their goal of a more just and equitable society.

Sadly, the Grand Old Party has since undergone extreme ideological changes. Initially, as you heard, it once stood for principles. Over the years, it has instead traditionally boosted big business with tax cuts for the ultra-rich. Yes, in our current political landscape, the GOP does stand for the Gas & Oil Project. Aside from the genuinely honorable, conservative Republicans, within the GOP is a growing body of despots governed by fanatical Nationalism, whose roots are embedded with the Ku Klux Klan.

Wide-eyed, Izzy feels nauseous, slowly sips her Chamomile tea, and sheepishly tells Finn, *"This is intense. I feel like the Mad Hatter who once asked, 'Have I gone MAD?' And Alice in Wonderland replied, 'I am afraid so. You are entirely bonkers. But I'll tell you a secret: all the best people are."*

Pondering what she knew was, without a doubt, this party was right out of World War II's Nazi and Fascist playbook. Again and again, they would do all they could to prevent history from repeating itself.

Democracy

*We have become not a melting pot
but a mosaic of different people, different beliefs,
different yearnings, and different dreams.*

~Jimmy Carter

CHAPTER 29

Dear Bridge Builders,

From my heart to yours, as we know, the democratic experiment is not a foregone conclusion nor a given process but a fragile system that requires constant vigilance. It is an incredible means of achieving social justice where everyone is included and can be a voice for the voiceless.

Let us respect history's lessons and know this is a time of turning the tide, ending the worn-out cycles of suppression, and allowing you, dear future, to live freely. Even in a world woven together by the threads of two primal energies — love and fear — the fabric of existence dances between creation and destruction.

Radiant and vibrant life pulses through every living being, igniting passions, dreams, and connections. This energy breathes hope into the hearts of the weary and inspires the simplest acts of kindness.

On the other hand, fear lurks in the shadows, an insidious force that twists perceptions and manipulates humanity's essence. It feeds on doubt and uncertainty, creating barriers that divide and isolate.

The media spins tales of catastrophes, politicians wield fear as a weapon to control the masses, and societal pressures create a cacophony of anxiety.

Corruption thrives in this environment, where fear is weaponized to maintain power, stifling the unlimited potential for love and connection. Fear is a darkness that seeps into individuals' hearts, whispering lies that breed poverty, division, and despair. It convinces people they are alone in a dangerous world where survival is paramount over compassion. Fear is a menacing force that distorts the noblest intentions and creates a desperate scramble for self-preservation, where love is sacrificed on the altar of anger.

My God, throughout history, ruthless power mongers, monarchies, and monks created years, decades, and even centuries of fear through inquisitions. This was a series of institutions within the Catholic Church that aimed to combat heresy and maintain religious orthodoxy.

The brutal Inquisitions involved various methods of investigation, secretive trials, and inhumane punishment, including the Medieval, Spanish, and Roman Inquisitions, all designed to root out any group not worshipping who the church deemed. My dire concern is the persecution vendettas from those way-back years will one day be reenacted.

Along with the Religious Wars, the Holocaust, Fascism, Nazism, plus far too many horrific purges to list, fear has long been used as a convincing deterrent for the lower, middle, and working classes to speak their truth.

Understand that because this Era is a major reset, it is the end of old cycles in which fear, anger and hate have ruled. Those governing classes unwilling to relinquish power will create civil unrest, laud ludicrous lies, and manufacture divisions; however, transparency and love will overcome them.

GRATITUDE

As we express our gratitude, we must never forget not to utter words; the highest appreciation is to live by them.

~John F. Kennedy

CHAPTER 30

Listening to the last recording, the sun rose; thankfully, they were both off work that day. Deciding to meet up after going to their separate homes to shower and get some sleep, Izzy asked Finn to meet up for a picnic lunch in the woods. After a profoundly restful nap, I recalled a vivid dream of what could very well be our future. I was amazed by its synchronicity.

Upon arriving at Izzy's and my unique place, we sat on her handmade quilt spread out on the lush green grass, each vibrant and distinctive, on a beautiful meadow surrounded by colorful wildflowers and a gentle breeze. The afternoon sun casts a warm glow over the scene, creating a magical atmosphere. The quilt adds a cozy comfort to the picnic setting, inviting us to relax, enjoy the day, and strategize efficiently.

The picnic spread is a feast for the senses, with various delicious foods on wooden platters and colorful plates. There are sandwiches made with freshly baked bread, cheeses, and vegetables. Fruit platters glisten in the sunlight, offering sweet and juicy treats. Savory pastries rounded out the menu. We can't help but marvel at the beauty of the day and the joy of sharing a meal. Laughter and conversation fill the air, creating much-needed relaxation and true joy.

In gratitude, I said, *"Izzy, thank you, thank you. This is a mercy meal; I have always been passionate about social justice and fairness. I could not stand the political corruption that plagued our country, and hearing what I listened to last night, I know I am called to right these wrongs. Life is such an adventure of the soul.*

I just dreamt about when my Gawni Gracey and I discovered a hidden manuscript and letters from our mutual cousin, Willow Rose Toussiant. This is an excellent time to tell you because the same tyrannical history is trying to repeat itself.

"Oh, Finn, yes, with everything so dark that we are experiencing, being with the songbirds singing, butterflies winging 'round the flowers, and the breeze is reinvigorating, please tell me about her magic."

I was honored to share my grandmother's timeless tales. She always reminded me through her Sweet, Sacred Storytime of Kahlil Gibran's wisdom: *"It has been said that next to hunger and thirst, our most basic human need is for storytelling."* Grace set in motion the brilliance of our enrichingly elegant and extraordinarily exquisite inner lives, where creative fulfillment dwells. She asks us to express ourselves lovingly, openly, and effulgently; to deepen our imagination, inspiration, and innovation. We are retelling old stories, not repeating them; instead, let us discover the rhythm of every person's story, regardless of race, color, or creed.

It has been said that next to hunger and thirst, our most basic human need is for storytelling.

~Kahlil Gibran

When my Gawni Gayle's mother, Eloise Fontaine Kincannon, succumbed to a massive stroke, I accompanied her on a five-hundred-mile sentimental journey. Receiving Eloise's cremains honorably, we organized her private Celebration of Life and were present for the reading of her *Last Will and Testament.*

While preparing the family home for an Estate Sale, we stumbled upon a hidden attic that had been sealed for decades. It was dusty and dimly lit, filled with cobwebs and forgotten relics from the past, creating a ghostly yet fascinating atmosphere.

Curiosity highly piqued, rummaging through the forgotten valuables, uncovering forgotten family heirlooms and artifacts, we were astonished to discover Gawni's dad's trunk, an ornate chest tucked away in a nook and cranny. To pry it open took a bit of effort; however, once we did, a treasure trove of forgotten valuables unveiled itself. We found a collection of ribboned bound now, yellow letters, fascinating family photographs, and a beautifully bound book that caught our attention.

The book was a detailed account of the Toussaint family's heritage, chronicling the lives of our ancestors and the trials and triumphs they had faced over the generations. Tracing their lineage back through the centuries, they stumbled upon the name that would change everything — Willow Rose Dubois Toussaint, apothecary, born in 1540. Intrigued by the mention of a woman healer in our ancestry, we eagerly flipped through the pages, discovering stories of resilience, love, and sacrifice that had shaped our family's history. This is only one of her letters and is very telling of our present times.

In 1570, Willow wrote, *"As ancient Storytellers, our tales promise to cultivate a more refined, wiser, and kinder humanity. Storytelling affirms that our peace mission holds the light of awareness, elevates, and serves our dearest humanity with love. Lest we not be remiss, the trend of this timeline is dynamically charged.*

In my Apothecarial, Alchemical, and Avatar eras, as described until now, betrayals, elaborate conspiracies, unfair taxation, oppressive restrictions, limiting curfews, ongoing battles, pestilence, and political control exercised on the general populace by divisive churches, both the Protestants and Catholics.

I scribed the following letter to our seven-year-old twin daughters, Abigail and Gabrielle, to preserve our storied history. As a child, my Aunt Martha, meaning "the keeper of the home," would tell me a story illustrating how misinformation mistakenly can become the truth through the generations.

She would brew us a hot cuppa of rose hips, lavender, and mint tea blessed by the sun and the moon. Stirred with mercy and sweetened with the honey of divine love, its exquisite elixir was medicine. In her enrichingly enraptured Storyteller's voice, she would tell me …

Once upon a time, a young student was assigned to a grand monastery to study sacred Scriptoria, the art of Scribing. Think of the elder Monsieur obediently, albeit slowly, touring him through the vast abbey, if you will. Room after austere room, each one functional and authentic to its assigned duties, was viewed.

In residence, the monks, spiritual brothers, worked silently in reverence, faithfully fulfilling ordinary obligations as piety and were considered Godly. The student was taken into the bowels of the monastery, where Scribes were focused on writing. Since it was before Gutenberg's Press, they copied and wrote pamphlets, books, and even the Holy Bible by hand. Being incredibly astute, the young man asked the elder, "Kind sir, what if the Scribe makes a mistake?" Horrified, how dare this impertinent young imbecile question the meticulous work of anointed ecclesiastics? His answer was an unequivocal, "Never!"

After a full day of gardening, cooking, and cleaning, the monks and the boy sat down for dinner. Without a word being uttered, the soup was supped, bread was broken, and wine was sipped; they retired to their rooms. As the old priory clock stuck midnight, a howl of great anguish came from the basement of the sacred Scribes. To render any necessary aid, every monk in residence, plus the young boy, dashed below. There, they found the elder clutching a Priest's Book of Rules, weeping uncontrollably. Through his sorrowful sobs, he cried, "The word is CELEBRATE!"

Aunt Martha continued, *"Remember, my darling Willow, the wisdom from your childhood studies that Jesus Christ was never a Christian, Catholic, Calvinist, or Lutheran, nor was Buddha a Buddhist or Muhammad a Muslim. These spiritual men came to earth as Messengers of Light, Love, and Spiritual Freedom. From era to era, suppression has existed, running as a backdrop in every generation's programming. And, as we know, nothing changes until something changes."*

Oh, my God, Finn... this is so true. Thank you; it is, indeed, synchronistic! And onto another tender topic: Please tell me about Blackwood's affiliation with your dad. This is a suitable time to discuss the horrific impact of other corrupt politicians who created wars for profit, such as the Vietnam War by Deception. There is so much to talk about, but first, I want to tell you about my Dad's hero, a Vietnam veteran named David, who extended and enriched his life.

MIRACLES

Anyone who doesn't believe in miracles is not a realist.

~David Ben-Gurion

CHAPTER 31

Dearest Son,

We know that miracles are an everyday experience if we only notice them. However dark my future looked; it could never compare to the journey of a miracle man who showed up in my life: David Cornelius Miller. His poignant story of being a Green Beret, Medic, and Paratrooper in Vietnam is one of resilience and the harsh realities of war. He was my salvation,

My prayer was to find a construction job and afford a decent place to live so you could come and visit. After cycling in and out of short-term group homes just long enough to either be accosted or robbed and my dignity stolen, gaining independence was my goal.

I am grateful to share the following pages from his journal, which he gave us in the support group he started. Read this…

Dav1d's Journal

Writing is medicine.
It is an appropriate antidote to injury.
It is an appropriate companion for any difficult change.

~Julia Cameron

Chapter 32

From a fine mist falling on my battered face, I awakened in a dimly lit jungle covered with dirt and debris; my immobile body was heavy. Where was I? As early morning's fuchsia and periwinkle light dappled through teakwood trees, I was dazed and disoriented. With the thick smell of gunpowder lingering in the jungle, fragments of memories began playing in a slow-motion slide show. Recollections before the blast flooded back, my Army buddies, the mission, and laughter before the chaos.

My unit was on routine patrol, or so I thought, when the unexpected blast of the Claymore mine, a deafening roar, shattered the afternoon's relative calm. I remember the moment vividly, the world exploding around me — a blinding flash, the sound of metal shrapnel slicing through the air, and then nothing. The force of the explosion hit my backpack and catapulted me into the air, and my body flew as if it were a mere feather.

Time seemed to stand still as the immense rush of a great wind had hurled me into a nearby tree. Oh, my God, the impact, a jarring collision with the trunk, knocked the breath from my lungs, and everything went dark. An excruciating pain coursed through my head. I tried to move, but my limbs protested as if they belonged to someone else. I had no way of knowing how long I had been unconscious. My body was a battleground of pain and confusion, and I felt every bruise and scrape; open wounds were oozing.

I could hear the distant rustle of leaves and the occasional chirping of insects, but the absence of human presence was deafening. Where was my patrol?

Although I attempted to call out, my voice was lost, swallowed by the dense foliage. It felt as if I had been abandoned, left for dead amidst the thick undergrowth and towering trees. There was only me and the oppressive jungle, a haunting stillness.

In those uncertain moments, I surveyed a deserted, eerie combat zone. Once again, I would like to know where my platoon could be.

My mind raced, replaying the moments leading up to the explosion and the faces of those brave men I fought beside.

Since a Claymore mine was designed to inflict maximum damage, I began to fear the worst. Dear God, no… had they also been caught by its blast and blown to bits, or much worse, had they been captured? I prayed they had escaped.

And then it hit me like a punch to the gut. I had lost my dog tags in the chaos, or what if I had been left for dead? My platoon would have removed them. These were more than just metal tags; they were my identity and family link. Would my loved ones receive the dreaded notification that I was dead, just another casualty of this brutal war? The thought of my family receiving that news shattered something deep within me. I had to get back to them.

Despite sustaining serious head, leg, and shoulder injuries, I summoned all my strength and determination to push through the pain. I forced my limbs to respond as I gently pulled myself upright. My body protested at every turn, but the desire to survive overpowered the agony. I took a deep breath, the humid air filling my lungs, and assessed my surroundings. I could not afford to linger in despair.

The sounds of the jungle were returning, but a sense of urgency came with them. I had to avoid any signs that would lead the enemy to me. I was acutely aware that I could be walking into a trap or, worse, into the hands of those who might capture me.

Determined, I tried to get my bearings to begin navigating back to our encampment, relying on my training to stay low and silent. Each step was a battle against my throbbing body; each rustle of leaves reminded me that I had to return to base camp, my platoon, and safety.

The arduous trek, traversing the treacherous terrain of Ho Chi Minh's trail, which every path bore this name, came at significant risk — all the while, I recalled the routes we had taken during our patrols. The jungle felt alive around me, and I moved with the primal instincts ingrained in me through countless hours of training and experience. I focused on the sounds of the jungle, the distant calls of birds, and the occasional snap of a twig underfoot.

Each noise could be a warning, helpful guide, or worse, another Claymore mine.

I forced myself to stay alert. With every ounce of strength I could muster, I pressed forward, fueled by the hope of reuniting with my platoon, desperation to see my family again, and to prove that I was still alive.

My heart raced with fear and adrenaline as I pressed on, each step a testament to my will to survive. The thought of my fellow soldiers haunted me. Were they searching for me? Had they been able to regroup after the explosion? I imagined the faces of my friends' expressions of concern, their laughter, and the stories we shared around the fire at night. I couldn't let them down. I had to find them.

After what must have been days, I stumbled upon a small stream. The sound of running water was a relief, a reminder of life in this oppressive jungle. I knelt, cupping my hands to drink; the cool water was refreshing against my parched throat. I splashed my face, hoping to clear my mind and focus on the task ahead. As I sat by the stream, I listened intently, straining to catch any distant sounds that might indicate the presence of my platoon or danger nearby.

Feeling refreshed, I felt a flicker of hope, the possibility that they were still alive and searching for me. I knew I had to keep moving to return to them. I followed the stream, believing it might lead me to a more familiar area or back to the camp. The underbrush around me thickened, and I had to push through the dense vegetation, my body protesting with every movement. I felt the weight of exhaustion, but fear of capture or death drove me onward. Suddenly, I heard voices in the distance.

My heart leaped, a mixture of hope and terror coursing through me. Were they friends or foes? I crouched low, trying to remain hidden as I crept closer to the source of the sound. Peering through the foliage, I caught sight of a small group of soldiers. Relief flooded over me as l recognized their uniforms. They were part of my platoon. They were alive!

Before stepping out of the bushes, I called out my name and rank. I did not want to be mistaken for the Viet Cong or Charlie and shot. Upon recognizing me, my Army buddies looked as though they were seeing a ghost. My worst fears were realized; I had been mistakenly abandoned for dead, yet I was deeply grateful to be alive. Together, my fellow soldier boys of war and I wept. Then we celebrated!

Since the Army had expedited my death notification to my family stateside, they were mourning the loss of me, their precious son, beloved brother, and dear friend. For a time, they were unaware of my survival. Being left for dead added another layer of grief and confusion to my story. However, when I could call and tell them otherwise, it was one of the most amazing days of our lives — on both ends of the phone, tears of joy, relief, and gratitude flowed.

The trauma of the experience was compounded by the military's failure to recognize the severity of my wounds. Instead of receiving the longer-term care I desperately needed, I was sent on R and R briefly to Australia. Since I was in high demand because of my exceptional medical expertise, I was returned to combat. The psychological and physical toll of the war continued to weigh heavily on me.

After the devastating Claymore Mine incident, when I was paratrooping on a night jump mission, I landed on an uneven surface deep in the jungle and crushed my ankle. To add insult to injury, it never healed and prevented me from walking correctly ever again. I was honorably discharged and returned home, unrecognizable to my folks. I was emaciated and even had to wear my dad's petite clothing. It was a significant departure from my once robust size.

My entire continence, attitude, and demeanor had suffered for the worse. My mother was deeply concerned and known to lament, "That dear young man is not my son, mentally or physically." Mom was right; I was not the same man. I never spoke of the horrors I had seen. I learned that when we sustain wounds and trauma, once we understand how to move through them, they can become our greatest blessings.

Instead of a Pearl Harbor incident, our steady intervention in Vietnam formed the ideological foundation of America's approach throughout four presidencies. Another jewel of wisdom is to study history: this is the only way to prevent it from repeating itself. We have discussed the patterns that, until broken, will be recycled. We were told we were in Vietnam to stop the spread of communism and to further democracy. Yet, in retrospect, it was all a fraud; it was nothing more than war's money machine.

Defeated, we returned home without the same fanfare of a parade or a show of gratitude that the World War II soldiers received. Vietnam's draftees had an average age of only nineteen. They were sent to slaughter. We experienced lifelong PST and post-traumatic stress disorders that were never treated and were burdened with guilt for something we never instigated. To have witnessed the horrors of that war was debilitating.

When discharged, I was dispatched to Washington, D.C. I was still in my Army uniform, back on my beloved soil. As a survivor of 58,220 American soldiers killed in action, 150,000 wounded, and 21,000 permanently disabled, the average citizen looked down upon us war-weary soldiers. As an example, while I was at Dulles International Airport waiting for my flight home, an ignorant lady spit in my face and called me a baby killer.

To numb myself to the ongoing traumas of war, I self-medicated. Alcohol was a poisonous prescription, and it followed me for the rest of my life. I had one opportunity after another offered to me; however, as a broken soul, I could not follow through. Despite my becoming a functioning alcoholic, my journey is not only a testament to how war destroys young lives but also a story of perseverance. After trying to return to a semblance of normalcy, to no avail, I am grateful for the random, silver-lined pockets that enable me to cope day by day."

"*My God, Finn,*" said Izzy, "the actual costs of war can never be justified; however, the rewards of those who sacrificed their lives are worth their weight in gold. I am reminded of the stories I grew up hearing of pre-war beauty and post-war devastation, not to mention the battles in between."

Izzy continued, "*In a time when uncertainty, fear, and upheaval reign, the transformative power of joy emerges as a promise capable of saving the day in unexpected ways. It can be pivotal in navigating tumultuous times. While surrounded by such bliss, let me tell you of my great Nonnas' World War II sacrifice. I will begin with my Bella, after whom I am named."*

Bella
Italy 1938

Peace cannot be kept by force.
It can only be achieved by understanding.

~Albert Einstein

Chapter 33

In the same era of worn-torn Europe, Izzy's maternal great-grandmother, Sophia Isabella, known as Bella, was a vocal advocate for freedom and democracy. As a professor at the Italian University, she courageously organized peaceful protests. This fearless woman was far ahead of her time; she stood up against Mussolini, known as Il Duce, and the Fascist dictator's oppressive regime.

While I was growing up, my Nonna Claire told me stories about her mother, Bella, who adored her precious daughter, Claire. Fond memories of my Grandmother Claire brushing my hair were filled with her memories of her mother.

Bella instilled the importance of choices, freedom, and the right to pursue one's dreams. This truth embedded itself deep within young Claire's soul purpose: being inspired to defend and stand up against all the wrongs was the mantel she carried. If not, evil would grow, becoming a root of bitterness that cultivates blame, which bears the fruit of anger.

Even though Claire was young, Bella wanted her to know the horrific reality of Mussolini's fascist ideology. The government implemented policies that promoted and prompted women to have as many children as possible to feed the regime and banned women's once-safe abortion choices. Such extreme patriarchal systems marginalized and restricted women's access to higher education, employment opportunities, and political participation. Bella assured her little daughter Claire that being a voice for the voiceless was a noble and passionate quest.

Embracing her precious Claire, Bella pressed a small charm into her hands and lovingly whispered, "*My sweet daughter, here is an Owl Totem given to me by my grandmother. Its nocturnal wisdom helps to transform fear into courage by believing in its mythology of being protected from being blindsided.*

Even more magical, its medicine enables us to express the sonnets of our soul song that sings of joy effulgently; they emerge from deep within our being. Regardless of nationalist agendas, our inner freedoms of peace, gratitude, and beauty can never be curtailed."

Claire recounted how her great-grandmother Bella was a bright light at the women's university. She emerged as a beacon of education and progress for women in the early 20th century, only five years before Mussolini's rise to power in Italy. This institution provided a comprehensive education that included studying classical history, philosophy, and the humanities, focusing on the Roman emperors and the ideals of figures like Marcus Aurelius.

Since history has a way of repeating itself, Bella's curriculum emphasized the importance of understanding the ancient Roman Empire within the broader tapestry of antiquity. Her students were encouraged to examine the complexities of power, governance, and moral leadership.

For example, moral leadership is exemplified by leaders such as Marcus Aurelius, Augustus, and Trajan. Her fascinating classes highlighted the lessons that could be learned from their successes and failures, fostering critical thinking and analytical skills among the students. Aurelius was a philosopher-emperor who played a significant role in the university's philosophical studies. His writings, particularly the "Meditations." were deeply explored, focusing on his Stoic beliefs and the principles of virtue, duty, and humanity.

Students discussed his timeless ideas on self-discipline, compassion, and the importance of treating others with respect and dignity. The university sought to inspire its female scholars to embody these ideals in their own lives, encouraging them to dream of a more conscious way of living.

Bella was dedicated to creating a University atmosphere of empowerment and enlightenment. Women pursued academic knowledge and contemplated their roles in a rapidly changing society. The institution celebrated women's potential to contribute to public life and social progress, drawing inspiration from the philosophical and moral teachings of the past. Women were honored to harmonize the family life of being wives and mothers with their academic prowess.

As the shadow of Mussolini's fascism loomed on the horizon, this women's university stood as a testament to the enduring values of education, humanity, and the pursuit of knowledge. It aimed to equip women with the intellectual tools necessary to challenge societal norms and advocate for their rights, fostering a generation of leaders carrying forward the legacy of Roman philosophy and the dreams of a more humane world.

With big-eyed interest, Izzy asked her Nonna Claire, *"What happened to her classes when Mussolini took power in Italy in 1922?"*

'Oh, my Darling, his regime implemented policies to reshape Italian society according to fascist ideals. The educational system was one of the primary targets for these changes, as the government sought to promote nationalism and conformity. Emphasizing the humanities and the philosophical teachings of figures like Marcus Aurelius faced significant challenges.

The curriculum was altered to align with fascist ideology, focusing on subjects that glorified the state, militarism, and traditional gender roles. The emphasis on classical philosophy and the study of humanistic values diminished as the regime prioritized the indoctrination of students with fascist principles.

Faculty members who promoted liberal education and critical thinking were removed or silenced. Some educators who opposed the regime faced persecution, while others conformed to the new directives to retain their positions.

The vibrant discussions of ethics and humanity that characterized the university were stifled and replaced by a rigid curriculum that discouraged independent thought. For the female students, the atmosphere became increasingly restrictive. The regime promoted a vision of women primarily as mothers and homemakers, undermining the educational opportunities that had been available to them. Women were forced to abandon their academic pursuits in favor of fulfilling traditional roles within the family.

The impact of Mussolini's rule reshaped not only the university but also the lives and aspirations of the women who had sought knowledge and a more humane society."

Bella's bold actions inspired many others to oppose his authoritarian regime. Since the agencies did not take kindly to Bella's defiance, one fateful day, she was arrested and charged with treason for speaking out against Mussolini. Despite Claire's cries, her family's pleas, and the villagers' protests, she was sentenced to death by firing squad.

The day of Bella's execution was etched into the memories of those who loved her. Bella's bravery inspired future generations to stand up for what is right and just, no matter what the cost. Even in the darkest times, hope always exists for a brighter future. Claire never forgot her mother's ultimate sacrifice for freedom and justice.

Izzy reminded me that history confirms that anyone who disagreed with Mussolini was tortured, imprisoned, or executed. Thousands upon thousands of individuals who opposed the fascist regime were murdered. Plus, the targeting of ethnic and religious minorities was a standard practice. Even after Mussolini's death, it took many years for Izzy's Grandmother, Claire, to be free from the nightmares of his reign of terror. She never has nor ever will forget her mother's sacrifices.

Claire made it her mission to honor her mother's memory by continuing her fight for freedom and cultivating a better world. She became a human rights activist, speaking out against injustice and oppression wherever she saw it. Claire carried on Bella's legacy of courage and resilience, never backing down in the face of adversity.

Bella's spirit lives on through Claire's beautiful daughter, the Actor Sophia, and her precious great-granddaughter, me. Taking note of her world history studies, they revealed how this pattern existed in all eras of historical takeovers. My grandmother, Bella, was my shining star who stood for integrity, strength, and honor in a world that emphasized virtue, duty, and the importance of the collective good over individual ambition.

Izzy spoke with conviction, "Finn, an ideal *society is rooted in moral integrity, self-discipline, and a commitment to the welfare of others. From then on, I focused on the responsibilities of leadership and the importance of wisdom in governance. May history be positively changed because of our bravery. Whatever tomorrow brings, I clutch to the ancestral owl totem." the power of being the difference."*

The Echoes of Ancestors
France, 1930

Our history begins before we are born.
We represent hereditary influences of our race,
and our ancestors virtually live in us.

~James Nasmyth

CHAPTER 34

I was profoundly moved by Izzy's great Nonna's brave story. Musing over the bizarre Mussolini's tactics of fear, torture, and death, I shuddered at the thought of a regime being repeated by present-day ideologues. I took a long, refreshing drink of the herbal tea she had provided, sighed, and told her we would not allow her Nonna's death to be in vai*n*.

We were tenderly baring our souls; Izzy asked if she could continue, now with her French great-grand-pe're and grand-mere Toussaint's tale of horror.

However, first, she wanted me to know the beauty of pre-war France and her legacy. Before the Nazis invaded and took over her beloved country. I nodded, of course.

From an early age, Mimi enchanted Izzy with tales of her idyllic childhood. Stories of wandering through the magical, enchanted woods and frolicking in fields of golden sunflowers in 1930s France painted a picture of heaven on earth. Camille, known as Cammie to her loved ones, had pleasing traits that Izzy had inherited: coal-black hair in a long braid and violet-blue eyes. This was an image Izzy could easily conjure.

In her mind's eye, she could see her Mimi, dressed in a floral yellow frock, skipping through a lush green forest with a wicker basket in hand. The sun filtered through the canopy of trees, casting a warm golden glow on the forest floor. Birds sang melodiously in the background as Cammie's laughter filled the air. She always spotted clusters of wild mushrooms sprouting among the fallen leaves and moss-covered logs as she wandered through the woods. With careful hands, she plucked them, identifying them with the help of a well-worn guidebook her grandmother had given her.

The earthy scent of the forest and the sweet fragrance of wildflowers created an intoxicating aroma. In addition to mushrooms, the French forest was teeming with other fruits and flowers. Wild strawberries peeked out from under the foliage, their bright red hues contrasting with the greenery.

Blueberries and raspberries glistened like jewels in the dappled sunlight; she reached out and plucked them. The forest floor was also carpeted with an array of colorful wildflowers — delicate violets, vibrant buttercups, and fragrant lilies of the valley. Bees buzz around, drawn to the sweet nectar of the flowers, while butterflies flutter from bloom to bloom, and hummingbirds paint the scene with their iridescent wings.

She continued her foraging expedition and reveled in nature's beauty and abundance. The simplicity and purity of this idyllic childhood moment in 1930s France captures a sense of wonder and divine connection to the natural world that remains timeless and cherished.

"My dear Finn, it is heartbreaking to share that my Grand'Mere's sublime, fairytale life would be changed within two years. This is what happened…

PARIS

*There is but one Paris, and however hard living
may be here, the French air clears up
the brain and does one good.*

~Vincent Van Gogh

Chapter 35

O nce Paris fell to Nazi Germany on June 14, 1940, only one month after the German Wehrmacht stormed into France, the peaceful and incredibly blessed lives of Master Chef Stephane Sebastien Toussiant, his elegant wife Solange, and their three beautiful children, all under the age of ten, were shattered.

The family home, a beautiful stone villa passed down through generations, was appropriated by a high-ranking Nazi officer Colonel General Friederich Werner, a ruthless and imposing figure in his crisp uniform, along with his glamorous mistress, took over the Toussiant estate and demanded that the family cater to their every whim. Master Chef and Mrs. Toussiant, fearing for the safety of their children, had no choice but to comply.

The once vibrant Toussiant family now lived in uncertainty in the basement of their home, never knowing when Werner or his mistress's demands would come or what repercussions they would face for any perceived slight. Their cherished home, once a sanctuary of love and laughter, had been transformed into a prison of servitude under Werner's oppressive rule.

Mimi shared that despite their hardships and humiliation, the Toussiant family held onto hope, finding solace in each other and the quiet moments stolen away from their oppressors. As the war raged on, they clung to the belief that one day, they would reclaim their home and their freedom from the clutches of the invading forces.

They also had a secret; they were leaders of the underground French Resistance Movement and in the perfect place not only to overhear but even intercept crucial Nazi Plans.

The cruel German officer's somber mood contrasted with the once robust and hearty atmosphere. Even though ever watchful eyes enveloped the Toussaint family, the tight-knit and brilliant couple working together, they smuggled crucial messages out by way of the delivery people.

Stephane spent long hours in the kitchen, preparing lavish meals for their unwelcome guests. He also oversaw the dining hall activities. At the same time, Solange was required to play host to an endless stream of arrogant German officers who once consumed excessive amounts of wine every night; their lips were loose. She took mental notes of names and places, which helped her endure their rude mannerisms, condescending behaviors, and pompous attitudes.

When she was not hosting under the unsuspecting eye of Lieutenant General Friederich Werner, she tended to the extensive grounds — under the guise of gathering berries and mushrooms for Stephane, the surrounding forest allowed her to pass coded communications to French envoys.

With tears in her eyes, Mimi recalled that the Jewish population, gypsies, black people, and especially the disabled were piled into boxcars like livestock and simply began disappearing. Their friends feared they were being persecuted, tortured, and even murdered by the Germans. It was not until the end of the war that they discovered the trains were how thousands of people were deported to German concentration camps, where many perished.

Mimi was honored to learn that the French Resistance movement emerged nationwide, engaging in sabotage, espionage, and underground propaganda to undermine the German occupation. Sadly, in Vichy, France, the collaborationist government enacted anti-Semitic laws and cooperated with the Germans in the deportation of Jews.

However, groups within Vichy France resisted the collaborationist regime and supported the Allied cause. The occupation of France by Germany lasted until 1944, when Allied forces launched D-Day.

The experience of German-occupied France during World War II remains a complex and sad chapter in French history, marked by collaboration, resistance, and the enduring memory of those who suffered under Nazi rule.

Mimi and my father are dedicated to upholding the memory of Izzy's great-grandparents. Throughout my childhood, I was brought up with the stories of their being brave hearted French Resistance Leaders who were among the 90,000 Parisians, six million Jewish people, and millions of disabled, elderly, and the ethnic cleansing persons of color who were tortured and murdered by Nazis during World War II. This is profoundly heart-wrenching.

Sacrifice lingers within Mimi's soul, a constant reminder of the atrocities of the past. Despite the passage of time, the wounds of her family's loss remain tender and raw. An unyielding determination drives her. She honors her great-grandparents' memory and ensures their bravery and sacrifice are never forgotten.

Every day, she keeps their precious memory alive by creating their savory sauces, stews, and soups, all from Toussaint's legendary French cuisine, their legacy.

Mimi encouraged me to remember that I came from a seasoned stock of bravery blessed by the courage of my ancestors' sacrifice. Therefore, I could be anything I set my heart to be. My grandmother's influence and enthusiasm for French cooking inspired me to become a classical culinary chef. True to my dreams, I graduated with honors from Mimi's alma mater. Like rich French cream, I rose to the top.

Cordon Bleu

Learn from yesterday, live for today, hope for tomorrow.
The important thing is not to stop questioning.

~Albert Einstein

Chapter 36

Izzy's unwavering dedication to her craft, meticulous techniques, and use of the highest quality ingredients are the essence of refined French cooking. Her culinary masterpiece dishes are not just exquisite; they are a testament to her commitment, igniting a sense of admiration. Meticulously, Izzy creates visually stunning and flavorful dishes. Her culinary genius knows no bounds; she creates and serves unforgettable, imaginative, and sumptuous dishes.

As Izzy presents her elegant entrees, the diners are awed by her culinary skills. Her dishes are a symphony of flavors and textures that is not just impressive; it's a testament to her talent and creativity, which captivates her most fortunate diners.

Chef Isabella is as enthusiastic about her career as her parents are about their artistic fields of excellence. Her mother, father, and Mimi are proud of Izzy and beaming with pride. They see in her a force to be reckoned with, and her diligence is impeccable.

Within three years of graduating from Le Cordon Bleu, Izzy was an assistant to a renowned chef at Le Merci. A meal at Le Merci is not just a meal; it is an experience offering a glimpse into the artistry and rich history of French haute cuisine. Was it more than a twist of fate when the Longwells graced the tables of her restaurant? In retrospect, it was meant to be.

Alex, a man of refined taste, ordered the Sea Bass with Saffron Sauce. This white flatfish was perfectly prepared and plated on a bed of seasonal vegetables. The savory sauce, a blend of high-quality stock infused with saffron threads, added a luxurious depth of flavor. Its spicy pottage was poured over just before serving, creating a vibrant contrast between the creamy golden sauce and the flaky white fish.

Amalie's choice from Izzy's impressive menu proved another testament to her culinary artistry. The truffle risotto, a dish that appeared more like art than sustenance, was a visual and gastronomic delight. With its swirls of savory sauce, bright splashes of color, and forms that felt confoundingly alive, this elegant meal was a true masterpiece that delighted Amalie's palette.

When the Longwells asked to meet Izzy to compliment her, they were immediately taken by her genuineness and charm and, of course, were already impressed with her culinary skills. Their admiration inspired them, as stated earlier, to recommend her for the prestigious Master Chef position at the Oakwood Country Club to follow the adored Chef Louis Leblanc, who retired after serving the club for thirty-six phenomenal years. And… the rest is history!

Genesis: Fund Raising from the Heart

A single event can awaken a stranger unknown to us, within us. To live is to be slowly born.

~Antoine de Saint-Exurpery

Chapter 37

The opulent Oakwood Country Club was a prime choice for the fundraising of Genesis "Gen" Wentworth, the female presidential nominee, and it was a much grander affair than Blackwood's. The venue exuded authentic elegance and sophistication. Luxury cascaded in stylish floral arrangements, crystal chandeliers, and black and gold accents, each detail adding enormous beauty to the fortuitous event.

Influential guests were dressed in exquisite attire, with the women wearing designer ball gowns and the men donning tailored tuxedos. The air was filled with anticipation as the prestigious guests mingled and enjoyed cocktails before being seated for dinner. The meal was a lavish five-course feast by the renowned Chef Isabella, featuring delicacies such as foie gras, lobster bisque, and filet mignon. Each course was expertly paired with fine wines and champagne, adding to the abundance of the evening.

As the dinner progressed, speeches eloquently supporting the first female presidential nominee, highlighting her achievements and vision for the future, were delivered. The atmosphere was of unity and empowerment. The guests came together to support a candidate they believed in. Overall, the evening at the posh country club was a stunning display of good taste, wealth, and favor for a bold, trailblazing female leader, leaving a positive impression on all who attended.

I am honored to have been Genesis's entertainment, singing Broadway show tunes from *Into the Woods, Hamilton, and West Side Story*. I thoroughly enjoyed attending her upbeat, high-energy soiree. Her smile was genuine, and she radiated unconditionally luminous love. I respected and was blessed to campaign for her and vote for her. The stark contrast between the arrogant Blackwood and the elegant Genesis was evident.

After my songs received an ovation, I asked everyone to please stand and join me in welcoming our first female presidential nominee. Humbly, Genesis bowed and began passionately speaking of her vision for our country and her plans to address the nation's critical issues. She articulated her stance on important topics such as healthcare reform, education, climate change, and social justice. The candidate emphasized the need for unity and collaboration among citizens from all walks of life, regardless of political affiliation.

She emphasized the importance of inclusivity and diversity, highlighting gratitude's power and strength and embracing different perspectives and experiences. She shared personal anecdotes that resonated with the guests, showcasing her empathy and understanding of Americans' challenges.

Genesis outlined specific policy proposals and initiatives that she planned to implement if elected, emphasizing her commitment to creating positive change and improving the lives of all citizens. The candidate's speech was inspiring and uplifting, instilling hope and confidence in her keen leadership ability, integrity, empathy, and sharp vision for a better future.

Her academic excellence led her to a prestigious university, where she studied political science, sociology, and law. After college, she embarked on a transformational journey with the Peace Corps, serving in a rural community in Central America. This life-changing experience deepened her insight into global issues, poverty, and the impact of local governance. It was a turning point that fueled her passion for public service and inspired her to make a significant difference in the world.

Upon returning to the U.S., she finished her studies and became a civil rights attorney. Over the next three decades of stellar contributions, she served as a state governor and then senator, championing health care reform, education access, and sustainable environment policies, earning bipartisan respect.

In a genuine voice, from her heart, Genesis shared: *"My career is a testament to resilience, marked by my unwavering determination to face tests, resolve challenges, and find workable solutions. From budget crises to natural disasters, I view these difficulties not as obstacles but as opportunities to learn and grow.*

My focus on dialogue, inclusiveness, and grassroots activism is not just a strategy but a demonstration of my toughness in facing adversity, a journey many can empathize with. My campaign is built on restoring trust in government and empowering communities with active, effective, and transparent policies. I recognize the challenges my predecessor's plans faced in the House and Congress."

She pauses and thinks of flashbacks that shaped her views and fueled her ambitions, reminding her of the millions of constituents. She wonders, "Do they think I am just another candidate? No, I am the voice of every parent who juggles work and family.

"Please do not underestimate me. When I stand on the stage with a thousand eyes on me, I reflect on those battles: I'm not just another politician; I'm a mother, a fighter, and the voice for those who feel unheard, unseen, and unsung. I hear you; I see you, and we will sing humanity's song together. These are our deliberate choices.

My internal monologue portrays the complexity and balancing of a campaign's difficulties in a raw, unfiltered manner. I sometimes, yet thankfully, not often, ask myself, "What am I doing? Am I enough?"

They say leadership is a performance, but I feel like a fraud every time I practice my speech. But then I think of my children, now adults, and I know I have theirs and our future generations to protect.

While I carry the privilege of potentially being the first female president, I am deeply grateful to have a solid moral code and to be known for my relatability and resilience. I use my platform to create better gender equality, social justice, and economic opportunity. These are my inspirations; I am here to fulfill my commitments. My story reflects a blend of personal and professional experiences.

For those of you who are just now meeting me, please know my family is a source of solace, grounding me amidst the stresses of public life. I have been married for over 35 years to my college sweetheart, Julian Maximillian Westwood. He is the love of my life. He is a distinguished historian focusing on ancient civilizations and their influence on modern society. As avid hikers, nature is our refuge, which reflects our commitment to environmental issues.

Looking around this room, filled with esteemed visionaries, I recall feeling terrified during my first debate. Yet when I saw my mother in the front row, her tears of pride made me see that this fight was bigger than me.

I openly express my frustrations about a broken system to illustrate my desire for positive change. The political arena feels like a glass ceiling that I am determined to shatter, piece by piece, not just for me but for every woman who dreams of breaking through. This is not simply political rhetoric but my belief system and purpose.

I know the value of education and how complicated tasks can help us become more vital. I have learned to evolve my struggles, or, as my dad would say, 'opportunities' with public perception, media scrutiny, and internal doubts, into high moral character.

I used to think that every negative article I read seemed to strip away a layer of my spirit, but then I remembered why I started this journey: for every woman whose voice has been lost in the noise. I am here to create a meaningful passage for all those who yearn to live freely and fully, all the while deepening their life journey just as I continue to do. We are in this globe together.

My long-term goal has always been to serve as President of the United States, a role that embodies hope and resilience. I understand the nation's complexities and the need for compassionate, pragmatic solutions.

My extensively successful experience and unwavering dedication to the American people make me a formidable candidate in a pivotal election. I offer a promising vision for the future. My Presidency will launch initiatives that guarantee funding for our schools, leading to a world-class education for all our children. We will create a task force dedicated to tackling crime and ensuring our neighborhoods are secure.

Picture a flourishing economy where jobs are plentiful, the perfect balance between creating clean, green energy, enhancing our health care benefits, and reducing student loans — don't you want to be a part of that?

I understand your trials — working families and dedicated business owners — and you deserve a leader who will fight for your interests. With your support, you are not just voters but integral partners. Together, we will champion policies that will lower taxes for hardworking citizens while bringing lucrative projects to prosper our nation. I will secure grants and investments that will drive our economy forward. Trust me when I say that with your contributions and vote, you will see your investments grow and be part of a legacy that will undoubtedly benefit all.

Can you Imagine investing in our communities? To launch initiatives that guarantee funding for much-needed infrastructure, reinvigorate manufacturing, and resolve immigration issues, we will witness the greatest economic boom since the 1880s when the U.S. economy rose at the fastest rate in its history, with real wages, wealth, GDP, and capital formation all increased rapidly.

Thank you for coming tonight. Your generosity means the world to me. With your support, I promise to bring about positive transformations. Peace to the world."

Everyone who attended this thrilling event left on a high note, inspired by the ambush on Democracy would be thwarted. In my theatrical thoughts, I picture our Shero Genesis as a distressed damsel tied up on a railroad track by the villainous Blackwood. As a speeding train is bearing down on her, as the caped crusader Superman, I rescue her and save the day. While Blackwood curls his handlebar mustache, he cries, "Curses foiled again!"

After Genesis received an overwhelming standing ovation, I was beyond inspired. I knew it was time to go to contact the Investigative Journalist and the FBI and play my recording. Knowing the plot to steal the election was well underway, I was dutybound to disclose that the fix was in. Tomorrow is the day! Indeed, Superman has nothing on me…

Lights, Camera, Action

True compassion means feeling another's pain and being moved to help relieve it.

~Daniel Goleman

Chapter 38

The morning after hearing Genesis's inspirational vision for our future, I stood on my townhome's balcony; the sun peaked from the horizon, painting the sky in red, purple, and pink hues. If only the tension and turmoil turning and churning in my soul could mirror the serenity of my surroundings, I would be more confident about going to the FBI.

Revisiting all that had unfolded, I was still reeling how Blackwood, a once-revered politician, had sold his soul to Big Oil and spiraled into corruption. He was actively siphoning off support for clean energy initiatives, blocking EPA's higher standards, and damning future generations to experience toxic, polluted air by way of greedy fossil fuel corporations.

The television news cycle highlighted his and the GOP nominee Dick Tador's visit to Corpus Christi, Texas, with their advisors giving them their undivided attention, which was scripted. A close-up of the candidate revealed his leering eyes glinting with deceit.

Behind them, a big picture window overlooked the skyline tainted with smog, a grim reminder that the environment was at stake. I knew Blackwood was soft-pedaling because, state by state, GOP Senators, also paid by Big Oil, were set to roll back the higher air quality standards and, eventually, abandon them entirely.

In addition, evil foreign influences and their plot to steal the election were on track to pull off their devious caper. Ironically, these measures initiated by conservative **G**rand **O**ld **P**arty members, admittedly referred to as the **G**as & **O**il **P**roject, would be the end of their existence.

Little did they understand that although they thought they were at the helm, pulling the strings of their puppet Dick Tador, the megalomaniacal Cabal was the true puppet master. They would soon discover their grave error in judgment.

Before going to the FBI, I emailed a trusted investigative journalist, Sheamus Samuel Kilgore. He is a seasoned reporter with an eye for exposing corruption. He has traversed the complex realms of powerful corporations and exposed their dark underbelly. His probes unearthed and made visible those who attempted to operate with sheer impunity and would stop at nothing to protect their unethical interests, such as big oil, digital currency, drug, and human trafficking.

Today is the day, with lights, camera, and action; genuine compassion is the star of this film.

Shaemus Samuel Kilgore

It always seems impossible until it is done.

~Nelson Mandela

Chapter 39

Sheamus Samuel Kilgore was experienced in uncovering sinister corporate espionage, those who were manipulating markets, and regularly engaging in hostile takeovers to eliminate competition through their underhanded practices.

His current focus is a sect of billionaires whose illicit world involves mishandling political systems. Their wealth influences high-level elections, giving them significant leverage to lobby toward their favorable legislation via political campaigns through secretive super PACs and accumulating even more resources through unethical schemes.

As Shaemus diligently pieced together the threads of his riveting story, his life took a precarious turn. He received anonymous threats warning him to back off. The more he dug, the more he felt the chill of danger creeping closer. His instincts told him he was a foremost risk to the sinister corporations. Determined to uncover the truth, he pressed on, knowing that his pursuit of justice might cost him everything.

To fund political campaigns that serve their interests at the expense of the public good, the Cabal created shadow organizations and think tanks that spread propaganda by way of disinformation, distorted public perception, and significantly undermined democracy. They even stooped so low as to spread devastating lies during tragic events such as apocalyptic fires, historical flooding, tornadic disasters, and harrowing hurricanes.

Environmental degradation is one of their significant areas of concern, with billionaires investing in industries that exploit natural resources without regard for sustainability, a complete disregard for climate change, and ecological destruction.

Additionally, these elitists operate with a complete lack of accountability, where whistle-blowers are silenced through financial powers and intimidation, which creates a climate of fear.

The vast divide between wealthy elites and average citizens leads to social unrest and a growing distrust in institutions. Sheamus's noble quest for justice and transparency has become a dangerous endeavor, with the stakes involving financial ruin, personal safety, and freedom. However, he is dedicated to these causes.

Shaemus discreetly managed explosive information as he was the nephew of a respected reporter, murdered in a car bombing for disclosing corrupt land deals being sold to the federal government. In secrecy, he brought the case of the five fraudulently involved Senators, including Blackwood. Sadly, they all skirted justice; were never prosecuted for insider trading, yet they profited in the millions. However, Shaemus never lost sight of this travesty and continued to honor his beloved uncle's memory.

After a particularly pressured-driven day of evading conspicuous surveillance, receiving menacing texts, and dealing with the consequences of his revelations, Sheamus sat down at one of his favorite places in the universe, his antique Oak desk, a gift from his grandfather Samual.

He opened his laptop, the cursor blinking steadily, and saw a familiar name in his inbox: Finn Kincannon. He recalled meeting him at a Genesis Wentworth fund-raising dinner at the prestigious Oakwood Country Club. Finn, a gifted singer, had been the evening's entertainment.

Finn said it was most urgent that they meet. But why and where? Being surveilled presented a challenge, yet over the years, he had slipped by the best of them. Cloak-and-dagger work was simply part of the job. Fortunately, when he purchased his condo from the generous proceeds of his bestselling book, *The Hidden Game of Navigating Corporate Espionage,* he installed a secret side door just for this circumstance. He could easily slip out and quickly be in the alley unnoticed.

Since Finn's email piqued his curiosity, he dashed off a reply, "Meet me at the downtown Daily Grind Café by the square at noon. Be careful I am being followed!"

Arriving early, true to his caution to be careful, I noticed an SUV parked at the curb, the engine idling with an ominous hum. Is this

Shaemus's surveillance? If so, how did they know where he would be going beforehand? For a moment, I hesitated, my instincts screaming for me to turn back. Yet, it was imperative to reveal Blackwood's treasonous plot, the foreign influences' planning to steal the election, and my smoking gun, the recorded information, to him and then to the FBI. The moment was now.

Once inside the café, I quickly sat down in a back booth, scanning the room for any signs of unusual scrutiny. My gut was still twisted with apprehension. I waited for Sheamus to arrive and asked myself, *"How did I get cast in this cloak-and-dagger noir film? Was I Hercule Perot or Sam Spade? Or even better, "Of all the gin joints in all of the towns and all of the world…"* The surreal circumstances had led me to this point in time. I had to admit I was all in.

Shaemus, an athletic man in his late fifties whose youthful appearance belied his age, was crowned with silver-streaked red hair. With his ivory-colored crew neck tee-shirt, he wore a root beer brown corduroy jacket, befitting his scholarly reputation for flawless research. His confident gait is complemented by Levi 501s and his classic penny loafers, which he wore sockless. As he approached, I detected a hint of Tom Ford's F***ing Fabulous cologne.

He recognized me from Genesis's fundraiser and, to confirm, asked if I was Finn. *"Yes, I am. Thank you for coming, and please take a seat. I have taken the liberty of ordering us a coffee. How do you take yours, black or with cream?"*

In a hushed voice, I told Shaemus, *"I understand you have experienced Blackwood's deceitful deception's up close and personal. Join the club. Under the table, I am handing you a copy of a recording that I secretly made of his conversations with powerful people. It spells out his corrupt plans to dismantle democracy. You will also hear even more condemning information about the foreign influences plotting to steal our presidential election. Plus, it lays out their use of the notorious liar, Dick Tador, the Court Jester. He is also a Puppet, a Pawn, a Joker, and a Wanna-be King. His empty promises will be his legacy."*

The Daily Grind

Coffee, the favorite drink of the civilized world.

~Thomas Jefferson

CHAPTER 40

O rinking his black coffee, Shaemus listened intently to Finn and replied, "*You have something important here, and I can see you understand the gravity of what you have uncovered. This is not just a story but a bombshell that could shake the foundations of power. But let me be clear: please be careful. You have crossed the line of no return and are now positioned as a loose end in a dangerous game.*

They will not take kindly to anyone threatening their interests, especially someone with evidence that could expose them. You are not just a whistleblower; you are a target. I admire that you may think you are doing the right thing, but you must consider the risks. Please keep your head down. Trust is a luxury you cannot afford right now. It would not hurt to consider your safety first, even as you fight for what is right.

You confirm my long time suspicion that a direct link exists between Oakwood Country Club and the Cabal, who are even more potent than Blackwood. What you have recorded is profound.

The truth is powerful, but it also makes you vulnerable. Be smart about how you proceed. Share your information carefully, and do not let anyone know how much you know. They will come for you when they realize you are a threat. Just remember, you are not alone in this. If we play it right, we can shine a light on what is happening, but you must protect yourself."

Waxing philosophically, I told Shaemus how tragic it is that millions of people are being conned. It is a bait-and-switch political ploy that says one thing yet does one hundred eighty degrees of the opposite. I know the time will come when those voters realize they have inadvertently supported oligarchs, billionaires, and corrupt politicians.

I know you understand this is an atypical, undulating political landscape. However, when well-intentioned citizens do not achieve the life they hoped for, have significant setbacks, or cannot get ahead, it is easier for some people to blame someone else for their problems, especially the government. I am dismayed that people do not understand that we live in an abundant country where our freedom to advance is always due to our efforts.

I believe that life experiences enrich and teach us valuable lessons. They are all about resetting and not regretting. We are in a pivotal time of transformation; indeed, the winds of change are upon us. Let us initiate favorable societal policies that do not burden us with governmental overreach yet evolve the quality of our living standards, elevate health care, and create direct access to educational opportunities.

We must be diligent regarding human rights. Thank you for taking me seriously. When Shaemus stood to take his leave, his firm handshake changed into a bear hug. Sincerely, he said, *"Since you are the same age as my daughter, I feel a fatherly connection with you. She is also a passionate person.*

To learn more about you, I pulled up any newspaper articles referencing your name. I discovered an article about your dad and downloaded it: Finnegan Padraig "Paddy" Kincannon's obituary. I am sure that you have crossed paths with Blackwood before. I imagine this quest is your destiny and is much more complicated.

Finn, I have permission from another whistleblower to tell you of his ongoing mission to expose Blackwood. You met him as one of the dinner party guests; he is Jackson 'Jax' Joseph. Several years ago, I worked with him on an environmental fraud case that vindicated and even saved thousands of lives and incarcerated the perpetrators — well, all except Blackwood; go figure.

Jax has been undercover on Blackwood's advisory staff ever since. He is an inside man of integrity who holds his own in a snake's den. Effortlessly, he navigates through their murky waters of deception. The case we built was based on the corruption of corporate waste, their toxins being dumped into aquifers that contaminated streams, waterways, and lakes. Sadly, these were in lower-income communities, and the cancer clusters that resulted were devastating.

Finn, you have done more than enough. I will take it from here and promise to inform you about my progress. Even though you are a brave young man, you still must take my warnings to heart. These ruthless characters crave power and will not let anything, or anyone stand in their way. Watch your back!"

"Shaemus, Yes, you are correct regarding Blackwood. Twenty years ago, he shattered my dad's chances and thousands of others in need of mental health assistance for recovery. His shady dealings cost lives. I am in your debt; thank you. I will be careful."

Shaemus left before me; I texted Izzy to let her know my meeting exceeded my expectations. I am on my way to the FBI. I have so much to tell you at tonight's teatime. See you then.

FBI

*Here's what I believe: I think the FBI is the premiere
law enforcement agency in the history of the world,
but I think there was some bad apples over there.*

~John Fitzgerald Kennedy

Chapter 41

1 was apprehensive, yet I followed through and went to the FBI to give them a copy of the recordings. As I walked into the sterile, intimidating lobby of the FBI building, my heart raced as fast as it did when I first ran to tell Izzy about the plot to overthrow our democracy.

With a mix of fear and determination, I approached the desk, where a receptionist looked me over with a practiced, disinterested gaze. I asked to speak with the top investigator regarding crimes being perpetrated against the United States.

My actions were driven by a deep understanding of this mission's importance; she perceived enough to know this situation was urgent. I got her attention.

After I showed proof of identification and waited a brief time, I was led through a series of locked doors with security checkpoints. My anxiety coiled tighter in my stomach with each step. Finally, I found myself in a small interrogation room with a single table, three chairs, and a glaring overhead light. The door opened, and Agent Agatha Christina 'Christi" Collins stepped in; the irony is not lost on me!

She is in her late thirties, clad in a crisp white blouse and a navy-blue pencil skirt that conveys authority. Sharp featured, she has the same piercing blue eyes as mine. She analyzed me from the moment she walked in. Her dark hair is pulled back in a no-nonsense bun, and she is professional.

High ranking agent Agatha Christi sets a briefcase down on the table with a deliberate thud, her movements precise and controlled. She introduced me to one of her interns. She sits, her posture straight, exuding an air of skepticism. As she begins to question me, the warmth in her voice is overshadowed by the coldness of her gaze. She leans forward slightly, a hint of challenge in her demeanor. *"What exactly do you think you have?"* she asks, her tone suggesting that she already doubts the validity of my claims. Every word is measured, and I can feel the weight of her suspicion.

As I recount my experiences of what I overheard and the dreams that have since haunted me, I notice her expression is hardening.

She interrupts me, her brow furrowing; I realize she sees me not as a bold whistleblower but as a potential traitor. *"You have to understand how this looks,"* she asserts, her voice firm. *"A private citizen claiming to know about a conspiracy involving high-ranking officials raises red flags."* My dismay deepens as I see the steel in her eyes. I try to communicate my sincerity and genuine fear for our country, but she seems more interested in the implications of my involvement.

The questions grow more pointed, almost accusatory. *"What evidence do you have? How do we know you are not part of this plot?"* Each accusation feels like a blow, and I struggle to articulate my innocence.

I never imagined reporting the perpetrators' plots and plans would lead me into a web of suspicion, where I feel like a criminal instead of a redeeming quality. As the interrogation continues, I must convince Agent Agatha Christi that my motives are pure. I want her to uncover the truth behind the politicians' machinations before it becomes too late.

With resolve, I lean forward, desperation creeping into my voice as I plead my case. I recount the details of my position as Oakwood Country Club's head server, where I overheard Senator Blackwood blatantly recruit other billionaires to join his covert plans. I have not only had recurring dreams, more like nightmares, of his devious plot to overthrow our precious yet fragile democracy, but I recorded it.

I emphasized that I am not seeking fame or fortune; I only want to protect my country from the darkness I believe is looming.

Agent Agatha Christi remains stoic, her expression unyielding. She taps a pen against her notepad, echoing in the small room. *"You need to understand the gravity of what you're claiming. These are powerful individuals who do not take kindly to accusations like yours. What if you are wrong? What if you are a paranoid citizen projecting fears onto innocent people?"*

My heart sinks at her implications, but I press on, trying to connect my recurring dreams with reality. I divulge specific events I have seen and how they align with current political moves. I describe a recent bill pushed through Congress that fits the patterns I witnessed in my dreams.

I see a flicker of interest in her eyes, but it quickly vanishes as she regains her composure. She warns, her voice steady, yet there is an underlying tension. *"You understand that if we pursue this and it turns out to be false, the consequences could be severe for you."*

I take a deep breath to maintain my composure despite the mounting pressure. *"I'm willing to take that risk. I know what I saw. I can help you uncover the truth."*

She studies me again, her gaze piercing. I can sense the conflict within her, between her duty as an agent to follow protocol and her instincts telling her there might be more to my story. *"Let's say for a moment that you're telling the truth,"* she says slowly. *What's your plan? How do you propose we investigate this?"*

Without drawing unwanted attention at that moment, a spark of hope ignites within me. I outline a strategy, suggesting discreet surveillance and reviewing the politicians' recent activities. I discuss building a case and gathering evidence to substantiate my claims without putting myself in the fire.

She watches me intently, her expression softening just a fraction. *"I will do a background check on you. To proceed, I must determine that you are not a liability. This is not a game, and if you are found to be deceptive, I cannot protect you."*

I nod, understanding the stakes. I am not just fighting for my credibility; I am fighting for the truth and my country. As I begin her process, I see the gears turning in her mind, weighing the risks against the potential rewards. After what feels like an eternity, she glances at me, her expression unreadable. *"I'll give you a chance. But it would be best if you were completely honest with me going forward. If I find one ounce of deceit, I will ensure you will be the first person we look into, and I will not hesitate to charge you. Now that you know the implications, are you sure you want to continue?"*

I did not hesitate and said, *"Absolutely!"*

Relief washed over me, but it was quickly tempered by the knowledge that I was now in a precarious position. I must prove myself to her; I believe the system designed to protect our country is in grave danger.

The conversation shifts as she asks questions about the people I overheard and who I have seen in my dreams. I described each in detail, recalling their mannerisms and the subtle power plays I observed.

Agent Agatha Christi takes notes and starts to piece together the narrative I am providing. As the hours pass, we begin to establish a tenuous trust. I can sense her trenchant skepticism is growing into curiosity. Her inquiries become sharper, pushing me to reveal more about my intimations, insights, and connecting dots that I had not considered.

When the session ends, she stands and gathers her things and says in a mixed tone of professionalism and urgency, *"I will need to corroborate your information. I expect you to remain available for follow-ups. This is not just a case; it is a potential national threat,"* I watch her leave, the door clicking shut behind her. I feel a surge of determination and understand I have stepped into a dangerous game. However, I also know that I am not alone anymore; the link between my recurring dreams and the reality of the ongoing conspiracy is clear.

The Chase

*Perception and reality are vastly disparate —
the truth somewhere in between.*

~Elle Kennedy

CHAPTER 42

As I exit the building, I feel the world's weight on my shoulders. I am on a mission to uncover the truth, prove my innocence, and stop a plot that could tear the government apart, a precious yet fragile democracy. The nightmares I once feared have become my only guide, and I am prepared to face whatever comes next.

A chill runs down my spine as I leave the FBI building. The late afternoon sun casts long shadows on the pavement, but the black SUV across the street catches my eye. It differs from the vehicle following Shaemus; however, tinted windows make seeing who or what might be inside impossible, and dread washed over me.

I brush off the feeling at first, telling myself it's just paranoia. But as I walk toward my car, I cannot shake the sensation of being watched. The SUV's engine hums quietly, and I notice it gently pulling away from the curb, trailing me at a distance.

Once again, my heart races as I try to remain calm. I take three turns, weaving through the city streets, hoping to shake off my unseen follower. But every time I glance back, I see that the SUV maintains a steady distance. Could it be someone from the FBI?

At first, I dismissed it as a coincidence in the busy city streets. What if days turn into weeks and the familiar silhouette, a black SUV, its tinted windows reflecting nothing but darkness, continues to follow me? With every sighting, I feel my throat tighten, and the pulse of fear quicken. If it were the agency, their surveillance tactics would be sophisticated, and their experience was evident. They sought to intimidate me, but I relentlessly pressed on.

As dusk fell, I sat at my kitchen table, drinking a cup of Earl Grey tea, the glow of my laptop illuminating pages filled with proof of Blackwood's illicit activities. I knew I had to make my recording public and publish my evidence before it was too late — before they tried to silence me. My unwavering courage in such danger was a testament to my resilience.

This was playing out just like my dreams, where I was at the mercy of an agency or whoever was surveilling me. Knowing they were experts at suppression, it was fair to assume, just like my nightmare foretold, their first move was to tighten the noose around my proverbial neck.

Orchestrating maniacal, subtle happenstances — an awkward bump on the street, a fleeting shadow that turned around just as I glanced back, and a whispered warning from a barista who handed me my morning coffee, *"We are watching you."*

Each encounter would be a message, a reminder that I was being scrutinized and that my silence was expected, intensifying the suspense. I could not stay cloistered in my townhome forever and was already claustrophobic.

I must breathe fresh air; the best place is the nearby city park. I tucked my laptop into my shoulder bag, and off I went. After walking for three blocks, I saw the familiar SUV and could feel the figures in the SUV's eyes on me. With adrenaline coursing through me, I pushed forward, yet in a moment of panic, I ducked behind a large oak tree. I could not let them catch me, so I quickly assessed my surroundings and looked for an escape route.

I spot a cluster of tall ornamental orange trees, the perfect camouflage leading to a narrow alleyway on the other side of the park. It is a risk, but it is my best option. I take a deep breath and dart through the crowds, weaving between people. As I force myself through the trees, I scrape my arms on the thorny branches. I stumble into the alley; I hear the park sounds behind me. The distant sounds of laughter and children playing starkly contrasted with the tense situation I hoped to have escaped.

I lean against the cool brick wall of the alley, peering back toward the park entrance. The SUV is still there, but now it is blocked by a line of cars waiting at a traffic light. I have a few moments before they can follow me again. Realizing I cannot stay in one place, I move further down the dark, narrow alley, littered with discarded newspapers and the faint smell of garbage. I keep my movements quick and quiet, instinctively staying low and alert.

I reach the end of the alley and spot a street that opens to a busier road. I cautiously peek out, ensuring the coast is clear before entering the light. The street is bustling, and I blend in among the pedestrians, feeling a brief sense of safety. I pull out my phone, fingers trembling, as I type a message to Agent Agatha Christi: "I think I'm being followed. We need *to meet… ASAP.*"

I press send and look around to gauge if anyone seems suspicious. With each passing moment, the urgency of my situation grows. I scan the area, looking for a place to lay low until I can regroup. A nearby coffee shop caught my eye.

A steady stream of customers offers a tribal sense of protection. The comforting aroma of coffee entices me to find a seat in the back corner, where I can watch the door. I ordered a coffee but barely touched it, my mind preoccupied with thoughts of the SUV and the figures following me.

I glance at my phone again, hoping for a reply from agent Agatha Christi, knowing that time is critical. If those in the SUV have ties to the conspiracy, they may already be onto me. After ten tense minutes, I decided I could not wait any longer. To prepare for what I must do, I pull out my laptop, connect to the cafe's Wi-Fi, and research the politicians I recorded and the additional ones I saw in my dreams.

Suddenly, I felt a presence nearby and saw a shadow looming over me. It is a barista, but I notice the unmistakable form of a man who stands just outside the coffee shop, scanning the interior with a predatory intensity. The barista holds a tray of coffee cups, unaware of the threat looming just beyond her.

Feeling the moment's urgency, I quickly close my laptop and tuck it back into my bag. I must get out of there before the man spots me. Glancing toward the back exit, I spy a narrow door that leads to yet another alley. It is risky, but it might be my best chance.

As I thank the barista absently, I head toward the back of the shop, moving as casually as possible. I pass the man outside and can feel the sting of the stranger's gaze, a sense of recognition that sends a chill down my spine. I push through the door just in time, stepping into the alley.

The stagnant air hits me, and it takes me a moment to steady myself. I know I cannot return the way I came; I need to put distance between myself and the coffee shop. I decided to head toward a nearby subway station, hoping to blend in with the crowd and lose my pursuer. I navigate the side streets.

The alleyway is dimly lit, yet I stay alert, ears perked for any sign of being followed. After five blocks, I arrived at the subway entrance. Descending the stairs, I feel a rush of relief. The bustling atmosphere of the station is alive with people, trains arriving and departing, and the echoing of rumbling wheels in the tiled cavern. I buy a ticket and board the next train, choosing a seat in the middle of the car where I can keep an eye on both entrances. As the train bellows along, I take a moment to collect my thoughts.

This situation escalates quickly, and I must ensure everything runs smoothly. I need to contact Agent Agatha Christi again, but I cannot risk using my phone if they track me. I got off the train at the next stop and found a public library. Since libraries have computers for public use and offer a quiet place to think. Still, gathering information without revealing my location or intentions is safer. When the train stops, I blend into the crowd, stepping off and moving swiftly toward the library.

Once I reach a computer, I consider what to search for. I want to learn everything I can about politicians from the recordings and my dreams, including their connections and recent activities that might further align with the conspiracy. As I approach the library, I take a deep breath, trying to calm my nerves.

The grand, historical building stands firm in its red brick structure. Its timeless arched entrance embraced me, and I felt like I was entering a portal of wisdom; I was grounded in its essence of consolation.

Inside, the atmosphere is quiet, filled with the soft rustling of pages and the tapping of keyboards. I quickly headed to the computer section and found an available terminal in a corner, away from the main entrance. Once seated, I opened the browser and began typing furiously, searching for news articles about the politicians I remembered. I recall their names, entering them individually into the search bar.

Thinking of Shaemus's words of warning, I keep my head down and fade into the shadows as much as possible. The results flood in, but I skim through the headlines, looking for anything suspicious or out of the ordinary. I discovered a plethora of articles, yet one in the Washington Gossip section discussing a secretive dinner party held last week caught my eye.

Due to its lack of public transparency, my instincts told me this was the one held at Oakwood. Reading the article and taking notes of names and dates, I try to remain inconspicuous. Yet I feel watched. I glanced around the library, scanning for anyone who might pay too much attention to me. I stumbled upon a forum discussing governmental conspiracy theories as I continued my research.

Knowing I must be cautious about the information's credibility, I cannot help but feel a pull toward the threads that mention Blackwood, which I have been dreaming about. My claims are evidence of unethical dealings and cover-ups, documents, and links that could provide Sheamus and the FBI with more proof.

Pulling my thoughts together, I realized I had not talked with my mother in days. I emailed her to sync up and confirm I would still care for Bruno, her chocolate lab, while she was about to cruise. I would see her in the morning before she departed and that I loved her.

Mom emailed back and told me how much she loved me, too. She thanked me for allowing her to take this fantasy four-month cruise worldwide. It was a dream trip on her bucket list that she had long looked forward to checking off. See you tomorrow. Love, Momma Joy.

EMERGENCY MEET UP

There is nothing so strong or safe
in an emergency of life as the simple truth.

~Charles Dickens

CHAPTER 43

My phone buzzes in my pocket; I pull it out cautiously, glancing at the screen. It is a message from Agent Agatha Christi Collins: *"Meet me at the Nifty-Fifty Diner on the 5th. I have information."*

A rush of hope surges through me, but it is quickly tempered by the realization that I must get there without being followed. I take a moment to gather my thoughts and decide on a plan. The diner is only a few blocks away, but I must be smart about my movements. Hurrying along the sidewalks, oblivious to my heightened sense of alertness.

I take a deep breath, reminding myself to stay calm and focused. As I approach the diner on 5th Street, I consciously avoid making direct eye contact with anyone, blending into the crowd as best as possible.

As I approach the diner's entrance, I push open the door and step inside. I hear the clatter of dishes, and the conversation grows louder. The restaurant is a classic, with red vinyl booths, black and white checkered tile floors, and chrome accents. The scent of bacon and fresh coffee fills the air, and clinking cutlery creates a comforting atmosphere. I enter the room quickly and spot Agent Collins seated in a booth at the back.

With concern and determination, I slid into the booth across from her. She looked at me intently, her expression unreadable. In a tone laced with urgency, I said, *"I think I'm being followed,"* glancing around to ensure we were not being watched. *"The black SUV. It has been tailing me since I left the FBI."*

She responds. *"That is not our SUV; our surveillance team would not have been spotted. I have alerted a few agents to monitor the area, but we cannot be too cautious."*

She pulls a folder from her bag and slides it across the table. *"This is what I managed to gather quickly since we last spoke. It contains information about the dinner party you mentioned and the guests' back-ground. Only Theo and Maggie Kensington stood out."*

I scanned the documents inside the folder, which contained photographs, articles, and notes detailing the connections between Theo and Maggie and some shadowy organizations.

The evidence suggests a network of influence that extends beyond simple political maneuvering. *"Look at this,"* she says, point-ing to a particular document. *"This is a transcript from a leaked phone call between two suspicious players discussing plans that match what you described in your dreams and the recording you played for me. They're planning something big."*

I felt a mix of validation and dread. *"What do we do with this information? We need to act before it's too late."*

Agent Agatha Christi explains, her blue eyes darting around the diner as if expecting someone to walk in at any moment, "First, we need to confirm the authenticity of this information. We cannot just take it at face value. If we go public with this too soon, it could endanger our investigation and you. I have an array of analysts who can verify the recording. We need to work quickly, but we also need to be smart about it. They might already know about your secrets if they are onto you."

Suddenly, a shadow loomed over our booth. A lady I recognized appeared beside our table, wearing a dark overcoat and designer sunglasses. She had an air of authority, but something was unsettling her. *"Agatha, your office told me where you were; we must speak. Now!"* Her voice was low but commanding.

Agatha stiffens, her demeanor noticeably shifting instantly. Surprised at the woman's unexpected arrival, her expression is unreadable; she turns back to me and whispers, *"Stay here!"*

I observe as she walks a few steps away from the woman. Where have I seen her before?

As they begin talking in hushed tones, bingo, it is Eve, Blackwood's damage control person. My God, what is she doing talking with Agatha? What am I missing? A sense of unease settles over me. I cannot help but strain to hear their conversation, but the din of the diner makes it difficult. I can see Agatha gesturing slightly, her body language tense.

I scan the restaurant more thoroughly, looking for anyone who seems out of place. My instincts are on high alert. Patrons are absorbed in their meals, but one man in a booth two tables over catch my eye. He is staring directly at me, his expression inscrutable.

A plan arises within me, and I contemplate the possibility that I have been compromised. I look back at the two women standing with their backs to me. At that moment, the suspicious man in the booth stands up and moves toward me. My inclination tells me to run, yet I know better; instead, I gulp and stop breathing.

The mystery man asks, *"Excuse me, did you drop this blue baseball hat? It looks like the one my friend Shaemus wears. You must be a sports fan, too."*

It took me a minute to process that he mentioned Shaemus; he must be a Friendly. Taking the cap, I saw a note tucked inside the brim and replied, *"Thank you. I thought I had lost it."*

Checking on Agatha Christi, who is still engaged in an intense conversation, I unfolded the message and read, Hey kid, just an old-fashioned note to let you know the guys in the SUV are mine, keeping tabs on you. I missed you at your townhome and did not want to call or text you. As you can imagine, destroy this note like in the movies; this one will not self-destruct, but we know this mission is possible. We are on the right side of justice; thanks for being one of the good guys, a true caped crusader. See you at your party this weekend to honor your Oakwood University Scholarship.

I wadded the note and slipped it into my pocket; Agatha Christi returned and sat beside me. It was perfect timing. I asked, *"I do not mean to probe, but was that, Eve Everhart? She seemed to make you very nervous."*

Agatha took a drink of her cold coffee and motioned to the waiter for her refill. *"How do you know Eve?"*

I answered, *"She was at Blackwood's dinner party, the one I recorded. I am curious; Agatha, how do you know her?"*

With a sly smile, Agatha replied, *"Finn, I would love to say, but then, I would have to kill you. You know I am just kidding, but seriously, this is something I cannot tell you at this time."*

Being the observant agent she is, Agatha noticed I was now wearing a ball cap, but she didn't say anything about it. I paused, considering the ramifications of telling her about Shaemus. Since transparency is essential, I pulled out the note, smoothed it flat, and handed it to her. This is from Shaemus, the investigative journalist I am working with.

She read the message and said, "*You have a guardian angel, and without incriminating myself, I know him to be especially trustworthy.*"

On that note, pun intended, I told her I must leave and meet a friend. Things are getting more interesting. Tipping my ball cap to her, I left feeling better than when I arrived. I assured her I would stay in touch.

To be continued...

WFTP

*Without strong watchdogs, and institutions,
impunity becomes the very foundation upon which
systems of corruption are built.*

~Rigoberta Menchu, Noble Prize Laureate

Chapter 44

I was excited to tell Izzy about Shaemus, Agatha Christi, and Jax. She, too, was thrilled about letting me know that Blackwood was hosting another dinner party, this time a fundraiser at his home. He asked her to cater for it, and she scheduled me as the head waiter.

We had time to organize this event properly. Could this be the divine opportunity we prayed to search his office for anything related to Sherwood? As we know, luck favors those who are prepared.

Musing over our late-night tea, Izzy asked what I told Shaemus about Theo and Maggie Kensington's WFTP, a television station morphing into a despicable platform. Along with hundreds of podcasts, blogs, and social media posts spreading hate, untruths, and downright fear, WFTP is the mother lode of despair.

As a respected investigative journalist, Shaemus suspected the link between WFTP and Blackwood. He gave me a copy of his op-ed on the station. I'll read it to you. Here goes: The once-respected WFTP, now known as 'Where False Truths Prevail,' succumbed to the temptations of power. This TV station was a beacon of journalistic integrity transformed into a tool for the GOP's powerful politician's agenda.

This makeover, fueled by Kensington's greed and ambition, began his platform's new era of corruption and ulterior motives. To his delight, he hired bigoted newscasters.

With a promise of funding and influence, the station's executives sealed a pact that would alter its purpose from informing the public to manipulating them. Little did their viewers know they were being used and laughed at behind closed doors.

WFTP was once a reliable source of information, yet at least half of the public watched in horror as the station descended into darkness. Its programming was now filled with sensational news segments that evoked negativity, elevated fear, and promoted racism, climate change denial, and immigration exaggeration.

Under Dick Tador's influence, it became an evil tool for spreading propaganda and focusing on bizarre misinformation, exaggerating and demonizing those who disagreed with them as if truth itself was a commodity to sell. Their focus was not a value or moral creed to live by. Stories of crime, economic collapse, and conspiracy theories became the bread and butter of their vile broadcasts.

Any positive news was either watered down, mocked, or completely ignored. Their focus was on sowing division, highlighting dissent, and presenting every segment through a lens of anxiety, ensuring that viewers stayed glued to their screens, feeling helpless and reliant on the very individual, Dick Tador, who had them in his back pockets and lined the station's coffers with newfound wealth.

Sweeping statements and comments by GOP-ers, such as anyone who votes blue is mentally impaired, were not only childish but, in fact, very telling of their lack of moral integrity. The viewers were trapped in a cycle of pessimism, held hostage by megalomaniacs.

The more fearmongering the viewers consumed, the more they perceived the world as dangerous. They turned to politicians and the media for solace — a symbiotic relationship of dependence that stifled critical thinking and fostered unquestioning loyalty. This corrupt alliance grew more profound as the broadcasts echoed in homes worldwide and were streamed on phones and laptops.

Trust in journalism waned while the politician's power solidified. Citizens became more polarized and less engaged in productive dialogue, feeding into an environment ripe for manipulation. Once a symbol of truth and honesty, WFTP station now served as an instrument of fear, forging a reality where darkness, depravity, and disillusionment thrived.

Shaemus's truth-telling editorial blew us away, I was stirred to share, "*This is the information the public must know. In addition to being in the newspaper and their app, he is on three podcasts this week. Isn't it a shame that Progressives are criticized as progressives? The irony is their focus, historically, has always been on the people, not the power. Everyone has the right to their opinion, but it is mine that unity is the only way to move forward. Our present political climate's division, blame, and bullying being propagated is heartbreaking.*

A person cannot live in a bog and experience love, peace, and harmony. Changing our environment and positively changing our mind changes everything.

PRESIDENT JIMMY CARTER

To be true to ourselves, we must be true to others.

~President Jimmy Carter

CHAPTER 45

*L*eadership is paramount to humanity and essential for us ever to evolve. Izzy, even though we have been focused on the corruption of politics, let me tell you about an incredible truth-teller, our 39ᵗʰ President, Jimmy Carter. He is honest, integrous, spiritual, and morally upright and would not be elected today. He is the antithesis of the Dick Tador and Blackwood programs, empty promises, healthcare concepts, and corruption. On the other hand, Jimmy was an honest, humble man of character, a peacemaker, and a visionary humanitarian.

In his 1976–1980 Presidency, Jimmy Carter advanced democracy, established a national energy policy, and founded the Department of Education. He decontrolled domestic petroleum prices to stimulate production and promoted climate change awareness, human rights, and economic and social development. Tirelessly, he worked to bridge the enormous chasm between the wealthy and the impoverished.

We must be inspired by his Habitat for Humanity, which built 350,000 homes and housed over 1.75 million people. Jimmy and his beloved wife, Rosalynn, worked side-by-side with tool belts strapped around their waists, hammering nails and sawing wood in their life-changing enterprise. They magnanimously traveled the world, demonstrating the gentleness of grace, tenderness of mercy, and the power of love."

Considering President Carter's incredibly fulfilling life and service, who fulfilled his destiny, and even Abraham Lincoln, who asked that our better angels guide us, I was deeply grateful to write the following journal entry.

As you know, my Gawni Grace teaches that we are the tales we tell ourselves. This is the alchemy of being a storyteller, scribe, shaman, and, as President Carter taught us, not only to be a prolific home builder; he was the quintessential Bridge Builder from conflict to peace.

For example, in his renowned Camp David Talks, he bridged an unprecedented peace treaty between Egypt and Israel. He demonstrated leadership at its best.

THE DANCE

When you think about quitting, think about why you started.

~Unknown

Chapter 46

Dear Bridge Builder,

This is a time when we elegantly waltz into our better selves. We are in an intricate dance between destiny and purpose, whose concepts often intertwine. Yet they hold distinct meanings that profoundly shape our lives.

Destiny is usually perceived as a predetermined path, a script written in the stars that we are fated to follow. It suggests a sense of inevitability, a force that guides us through life's twists and turns, sometimes leaving us feeling like mere spectators in our existence.

While it can be comforting to think that our lives are unfolding according to a grand design, I urge you to consider the weight of this belief. Destiny can make us passive observers, waiting for signs or signals to guide our choices; we are actively engaging in the process of living. In contrast, purpose is an active pursuit. The flame ignites our passions, so we leap out of bed each morning with a sense of intention.

Our purpose is what we create, not what is handed to us. It is the outcome of our choices, values, and desires. When we embrace our purpose, we take ownership of our narrative, weaving our experiences into a tapestry reflecting who we are. Purpose encourages us to explore, question, and grow. It invites us to look within and ask ourselves what brings us joy, fulfillment, and a sense of contribution to the world.

Understanding the difference between destiny and purpose is crucial. While destiny might set the stage, purpose allows us to craft our performance. We can choose how to respond to the circumstances that life presents. Our challenges can become stepping-stones, and our dreams can evolve into actionable plans. In this way, we are not confined by a predetermined fate but become the architects of our realities. As we navigate the complexities of life, remember that it is not enough to accept what comes our way simply.

Embrace the uncertainty and the chaos, for it is within that space that our purpose can emerge. Seek to understand what drives you, what you stand for, and how you can contribute to the greater good. Allow your purpose to guide you; in doing so, you may find that destiny becomes less of a constraint and more of a canvas upon which you can paint your aspirations. In the end, the journey is yours to define. Destiny may provide the backdrop, but your purpose will lead you to a life of meaning and fulfillment. Embrace it, cherish it, and let it illuminate your path.

Gratitude is a profound and transformative emotion that embodies appreciation for the people, experiences, and gifts that enrich our lives. It recognizes the goodness in the world, often prompting a deep connection to the divine. We embrace the idea that our love story is part of a much larger narrative that speaks to humanity's potential to evolve into something more significant. Let us walk forward with courage and grace, ready to embrace the universe.

When we cultivate gratitude, we shift our focus from what we lack to what we have, creating a space for abundance and joy. At its core, gratitude is about acknowledgment. It encourages us to pause and reflect on the blessings we often take for granted: the sun's warmth on our skin, the laughter of loved ones, the beauty of nature, and the kindness of strangers. This awareness opens our hearts and allows us to experience life more fully, deepening our appreciation for the present moment.

Practicing gratitude can profoundly impact our mental and emotional well-being. Research has shown that by regularly acknowledging difficulties with appreciation, even in the most challenging situations, we can find lessons and growth opportunities.

Gratitude also strengthens our relationships. When we express appreciation for others, we create bonds of connection and foster a sense of belonging. A simple thank you transforms moments, elevating interactions and deepening our ties. It reminds us that we are not alone in our journeys and encourages us to support and uplift each other. Moreover, gratitude is a practice that can be cultivated. It can start with small gestures.

Reflecting on the positive aspects of our lives can reshape our perspective, allowing us to approach life with a sense of wonder and openness. Ultimately, gratitude is a powerful force. It reminds us of our shared humanity and the interconnectedness of all beings. It invites us to embrace the beauty in the ordinary and honor the gifts surrounding us.

By cultivating a spirit of gratitude, we can transform our lives and the lives of those around us, creating a ripple effect of positivity and love. In this way, gratitude becomes an emotion and a way of life, enriching our experiences and guiding us toward deeper fulfillment.

Izzy refilled our teacups and thanked me, saying it was just what she needed to hear. With all the darkness we have dealt with, this is an illuminating truth: We are our storytellers and bridge builders. Like the Carters, let's strap on our transformational tool belt of joy, love, and peace and make a positive difference. Now, where do we begin?

OAK ~ GATE

I stay a little longer, as one stays,
to cover up that is still burning.

~Henry Wadsworth Longfellow

Chapter 47

Blackwood's Fund Raiser, a dinner party, was the perfect event to continue Oak Gate. We felt like Bernstein and Woodard; the possibility of uncovering Sherwood's deeply buried secrets was thrilling.

We counted our blessings; everything lined up better than we imagined. With that inspiration, it was a gift from heaven.

For the party, I asked Izzy, "*Do any themes come to mind? Say, like, 'Ay, Mate', what about a costume affair for buccaneers, bandits, and bullies? We can serve swashbuckling steak, rotten potatoes with rancid butter, and pizen' apple pie in 'me eye' all the while, and the guests symbolically walk the plank. Only kidding.*" Wink, wink! We laughed until our sides hurt.

From Shaemus to Agatha Christi, they were our better angels. We felt the synchronicity of being in the 'write' place at the right time. If everything continues to go our way, we will discover everyone involved in the Sherwood scandal — and speaking of hammering, we will drive the cue-de-gras nail into Blackwood's coffin. Shall we bury him at sea?

Upon arrival, as eerie as it was, I felt comfortable in Senator Blackwood's ostentatious dining room. Its mahogany furnishings, elegant accouterments, and an oversized, rather ostentatious chandelier spoke of his grandiose tastes. I am told he even has a gold toilet seat. This must refer to his secretive land dealings, as many real estate developers have preferred this type of throne. Oh, the irony!

Getting into the flow, I moved deftly between the table and the kitchen; my demeanor was polished and professional. With a clear mission, I was aware of the high stakes. At some point during the event, I would slip unnoticed into the Senator's private home office and hope to copy his files. Mindful that if any opportunity presented itself, it would only be a tiny window of time.

Izzy and I elected the catchphrase, 'The eagle has landed,' which would alert me to the slim yet crucial chance to fulfill our covert investigative strategy. We knew this gathering was not merely about raising funds, perhaps not as overtly absurd as the Oakwood dinner party, yet it would also have its secret agenda.

As I replenished wine glasses and served gourmet dishes, my ears perked up whenever I overheard snippets of conversation that hinted at something more sinister. Under my stylish server's apron, my phone was in record mode. I was listening for any discussions of backroom deals, money exchanges, and the mention of Dick Tador. Knowing he was involved in a highly mysterious and potentially damaging initiative that Blackwood allegedly used for personal gain. Any information that would reveal the Senator's additional corrupt activities was our goal.

Oakwood Country Club's damaging recording and ongoing investigations into Oak Gate proved somewhat humorous because when we abbreviated it, it was OG — not the original gangster, or was it?

Before his main speech, Blackwood wanted to say a few words to his guests between the salad and the main course. It was a gift from heaven for me to glance up and see that the Senator's home office door was left ajar. This was the perfect time to slip away unnoticed. Discreetly, I chanced to peer inside only to spy a sleek laptop left unattended on a desk.

After I confirmed that the guests were engrossed in his spiel, their laughter echoed from the dining room, and I knew this was the moment. Tonight was the time of reckoning. The potential danger of my actions added an extra layer of thrill to the situation. However, the reward could be monumental.

As I slipped inside, my heart was pounding. Could this be Blackwood's laptop setting here in plain sight? Eureka, it was indeed such a lucky break. Now, how would I log in? Thanks to a fortuitous, old-school sticky note on the side of the desk bearing the password, I felt a rush of adrenaline and typed it in; clicking the final key, the screen blinked to life.

What could I expect from an antiquated laptop? It was a dinosaur, making me wonder why he did not have a more up-to-date computer. As Blackwood's screen populated, I spied Pulitzer Prize-winning author the passionate and curious Edna Ferber's book cover, *Giant*. With its big Texas oil derrick, cowboy, and bucking Mustang, it was a message from the Universe. Yep, it was time to ride. I got chills.

Feeling like Wyatt Earp, a lawman closing in on the notorious outlaws of the Wild West, I worked urgently, fully aware that time was not on my side. My determination was profound as I navigated the dimly lit room; my only goal was to unearth the truth amidst the chaos of corruption. Finally, I was deep in Blackwood's highly sought-after emails; my fingers trembled with anticipation, and a plethora of files opened before me.

In the glow of his flickering computer screen, I felt like a lone ranger in a dusty town, where shadows danced like specters among the tumbleweeds. On a quest for the elusive file, a digital treasure hidden among the debris of a lawless frontier. The air was thick with tension, as palpable as the stench of gunpowder after a high noon showdown.

My heart raced like a wild stallion, galloping against the backdrop of a setting sun as I navigated the treacherous landscape of encrypted folders and firewalls. Each click echoed like the distant clang of a saloon door, a sound that could draw unwanted attention. I was not just hunting for evidence; I was tracking a rattlesnake in the grass, a deadly adversary lurking in the shadows, poised to strike. Pressure reticulated around me.

Sifting through the lawless files, I felt the weight of a thousand wanted posters bearing Blackwood's face. The clock was ticking, a relentless reminder that danger was just around the corner, like a posse of bandits riding into town at any moment. My instincts were sharp, sensing the threat of discovery as if the outlaws of the digital realm had their eyes peeled for any sign of a vigilante seeking justice.

With each passing second, I recalled the stories of brave marshals who faced the worst of the West, their courage forged in the fires of desperation. I couldn't afford to falter now; the stakes were as high as the mountains that loomed over the frontier. Finally, I spotted a file that shimmered like a gold nugget in a pan of muddy water. But even as he reached for it, I felt the chill of a breeze, a warning that the notorious outlaws were closing in.

The digital dust stirred around me; I had to act fast, like Wyatt Earp in Deadwood, drawing my revolver in a split second. At that moment, I was not just a man behind a screen; I was fighting against the tide of corruption, desperate to bring the lawless to justice before they could catch wind of my pursuit.

I opened the nugget labeled Eco Project and placed a USB drive into the portal; the download began: 10%..., 20%..., and 30%. It was ticking up in agonizing slowness. A faint whirring sound emanated from the machine, resembling a labored breath as if it struggled with the extracted larcenous information. Glaring in bold digits, the percentage counter flickered between numbers with fleeting motions of progress before it stalled.

Then, the unmistakable footsteps on the hardwood floor outside the door shattered my focus. The approaching sound of heels was like an executioner's gavel, sealing my fate with each echoing thud.

With the light on the laptop blinking, I stood up, smoothed my server's apron, and from the Senator's wet bar, I grabbed a fifth of Glenmorangie, the Lasanta Highland single malt Scotch Whiskey as if that was the reason for me being in the Senator's private office all along. Bravely, I opened the door.

Thank God, there stood Izzy. *"Finn,"* she cautioned, *"You only have five more minutes before you and Scott are to serve the main course. Plus, the Senator has asked you to sing his favorite song; you know the one."*

Each tick of the clock sounded like a drumbeat echoing in silence, amplifying the tension in the room. I wiped the sweat from my brow, my eyes fixed on the screen as the download paused at a meager 44%. Old Bessy flashed a message temporarily: *"Processing..."* followed by a spinning wheel that characterized a carousel going round and round while my old west carnival horse was going up and down.

In synch with the system's tormenting rhythm, the ambient noise from the dining room had faded entirely, and their once jovial chatter fell further away as if the world had shrunk to just me and this uncooperative laptop. Checking the time on my phone, I only had three minutes left.

The temptation to rush the desirous download was overbearing, as any hasty move could mean disaster. It was high noon, and my Wyatt Earp persona was at the O.K. Corral when suddenly, the computer emitted a soft beep, snapping me back to reality and emphasizing the dreadful silence. At this point, frustration and desperation were entwining. Finally, the machine's fan coughed to life determinedly to keep pace; the ominous light flickered as if it, too, feared being caught. My stomach churned.

With a low hum, the download resumed, inching forward to 53%..., 62%... each number felt colossal. The laptop's screen clarity was both a comfort and a curse; it kept me anchored within the reality of being caught. The transfer had danced between certainty and failure; a relentless pulse of anxiety mirrored it. With 30 seconds to spare, 71%... suddenly became 100%.

I removed the USB Drive, carefully opened the door, and peered out into the empty hallway. With a deep breath, I quickly returned to the kitchen. Izzy and I exchanged expressions of great relief.

In what could be Tombstone, it was as if nothing had transpired during my Wild West wisdom, "There was never a horse that couldn't be ridden, nor a cowboy who couldn't be thrown." Although this sagacity is unknown, it reminds us that setbacks are inevitable but not insurmountable. Confidently, without skipping a beat, I reentered the snake den. Per Blackwood's request, I performed one of his favorite songs, *A Rhinestone Cowboy;* it was ideal. No one knows better than these lyrics perfectly personifying Blackwood, "There's been a load of compromising, on the road to my horizon." I tucked my six-shooter back in its holster. Job well done!! It's time to serve dessert.

Master Chef Isabella's majestic torte has multiple layers of indulgence: a smooth and reflective ganache with just a touch of cream and a dash of fine Madagascar vanilla extract. Each bite brought a harmony of flavors, with hints of earthy truffles woven into the silky chocolate, elevating the experience to unexpected heights.

Garnished with fresh berries and a delicate mint sprig, the truffle is unforgettable and lasts until every morsel is savored. Starkly contrasting the tension of the previous moments, my mission cast a magical spell over the decadent dessert scene. I was ecstatic.

With the thumb drive safely tucked away in my pocket, Izzy and I pitched in with the wait staff, and we cleaned the and sang Toby Keith's "I Should've Been a Cowboy; I Should've Learned to Rope and Ride, Wearing My Six-Shooter, Riding My Pony on a Cattle Drive."

To unearth this treasure, we texted Shaemus to join us at my townhome. He replied that he would meet us there later tonight.

DESTINY

Furthermore, we have not even to risk the adventure alone, for the heroes of all time have gone before us. The labyrinth is thoroughly known. We have only to follow the thread of the hero's path, where we had thought to travel outward; we will come to the center of our existence. And where we had thought we would be alone; we would be with all the world.

~Joseph Campbell
Archetypal Scholar, The Hero's Journey

Chapter 48

Except for the Longwells and the Wycliffs, Shaemus, Agatha Christi, and Jax, who knew of Blackwood's corruption, we were being met with skepticism. Our family and a few friends were warning us about the looming political danger. Through the challenges and triumphs of our journey, we rose above doubts, trusted our instincts, and took decisive action.

At my town home, Izzy and I downloaded the Sherwood file. Clearly, destiny called our names as this experience strengthened our resolve, under-scoring the high stakes. While going through the transferred files, we were struck by the necessity of writing an exposé or, better yet, a graphic novel, changing the names of the guilty yet revealing the senator's myriad wrongdoings, including the hidden profits and the devastating impact on mental health services. We feel a rush of hope mixed with anxiety; this could be the opportunity when everything changes.

If the senator's camp learns of an impending book, they might start a smear campaign against us. Momentarily, I grapple with honoring my father's legacy; I question whether we dare to see this through. Within seconds, I knew this was the right thing to do.

Continuing our investigation, the Sherwood file reveals Blackwood's old emails and documents, leading us to a shocking discovery. We find a hidden file about the closed mental health facility, which contains notes and correspondence referencing a former patient who had been vocal about the facility's closure. Intrigued, we dug deeper and discovered that the patient was none other than my father.

Reading through the files, we learn that he had firsthand evidence against the senator and was planning to expose him. Piecing everything together, a chilling realization dawns on me: my father's death was not a suicide but a carefully orchestrated murder to silence him. Overwhelmed with grief and anger, I feel the ground shift beneath me.

We now realize again that our fight has been elevated to a higher calling. It is not just about exposing corruption; it has become personal. This revelation ignites a fire within us, fueling our determination to seek justice for my father and all the lives affected by the senator's greed. We cannot just write and publish the book without addressing Dad's murder.

Believing that our destiny is unfolding, we know that life is always for us. We are in the perfect place at the right time. Proof positive of synchronicity; the doorbell rings unexpectedly, and it is Shaemus.

Izzy brews one of her incredible pots of coffee, and while drinking in its exquisite elixir, we fill him in. He is unsurprised at our findings and tells us he is already facing a backlash by reopening the Sherwood Health Campus case. Explaining the new evidence and the potential danger we are now facing, he listens intently, understanding the gravity of the situation. We agree to include the story of my father's suspicious death, framing it as a crucial piece of the larger narrative.

As we prepare for this critical project, I feel vindication deep within my soul. Although bringing this information to light puts us in jeopardy, I understand that failing to act would dishonor my father's memory and the countless others who suffered in silence.

While creating our book outline, Shaemus received another anonymous warning to back off. We discussed the threat and weighed our options. Despite the risk, we cannot retreat now. We have come too far, and the truth must be told. Once the graphic novel is published, telling its story of corruption at the highest levels, it will send shockwaves through the greater community.

To boost our confidence and, indeed, to deepen our courage, Shaemus shared with Izzy and me the time he was about to release a story on religious leaders who were lording over their wives and children and who were being held hostage in their own homes.

Because of generations of programming, the wives and children did not even realize another way of life existed. I took meticulous notes, photographs, and papers that chronicled the web of deceit surrounding the religious leaders. I painstakingly pieced together testimonies from frightened victims, each more harrowing than the last. Their faces haunted me, a constant reminder of the darkness I was determined and about to expose.

One night, the tension thickened as I received an anonymous tip. A breadcrumb would lead me to a hidden meeting of the men I was investigating. I hesitated, knowing the danger, but the urgency of the truth propelled me forward.

Slipping into the shadows, approaching the clandestine gathering, I could hear hushed voices. Peering through a crack in the door, I saw these despicable figures cloaked in ominous authority, their faces illuminated by the flickering glow of hundreds of candles. Wearing ritualist red robes and massive silver crosses hanging from their necks, they were a sect, an offshoot of evil's hierarchy. The cult leader spoke of their control, influence, and the lengths they were willing to go to protect their secrets.

My hardened nerves of steel quickened as I realized I was witnessing a dark rite of power and manipulation. Pulling out my phone, I snapped a photo of these heartless men in the very throes of their depravity. Suddenly, a sharp noise shattered the quiet, and I stumbled back, knowing I had to retreat quickly, but hands grabbed me from behind as I turned.

I found myself face to face with a group of merciless men, their eyes cold and calculating. *"You should have stayed away,"* one of them hissed. They knew who I was, and at that moment, the reality of my situation sank in. Even though they thought they were untouchable, I refused to be silent in their twisted chess game.

Ramming into my offender, I managed to throw him off balance. In the nick of time, I spotted a fire alarm, pulled it, and ran like hell. My Irish luck was with me. I found safety in an adjacent building when a large conference ended, and I blended into the crowd — breathing in a deep sigh of relief. Gratefully, I entered the night's cool air that calmed me.

Returning home, understanding there was no time to be wasted, I urgently gathered all the evidence and took it to my longtime friend, the State Attorney General. After showing him the previous night's clan photo, warrants were obtained, arrests were made, and perpetrators were taken into custody. Once they were convicted, I took a long-earned vacation.

Hearing Shaemus's experiences of overcoming evil inspired us. There is so much to say about trusting our intentions; as Joseph Campbell taught, "Follow your bliss and do not be afraid, and doors will open where you didn't know they were going to be."

I reminded Izzy and Shaemus how Alex Longwell challenged Blackwood to look into his grandchildren's faces and explain why he sold his soul to Big Oil, which is cataclysmic to climate change and is undoubtedly our number one concern. He is bowing down to billionaire megalomaniacs and is perpetuating the power-crazy and vacuous Dick Tador's bid for the highest office in the land. His past swindling of projects such as Sherwood, fraudulent land grabbing, and waterways pollution are only scratching the surface.

An Oxymoron:
Blackwood's Consciousness

An oxymoron is a set of contradictory words whose rhetoric expresses a verbal puzzle, such as humor, drama, and irony. Such an honest politician calculated risk, controlled chaos, and accidentally on purpose, accurate estimates, bittersweet, and the same difference.

Chapter 49

Spellbound, we listened to Shaemus' experience, which not only relieved us but also warned us about the dangers of our project and prepared us for what we might face. We prayed our outcome would be as rewarding as his.

The book isn't just about the climate catastrophe caused by Blackwood's abolishment of the EPA, the closure of the Department of Education, and far too many to list that are now at risk, the foreign disinformation, and now includes the details of the Senator's corruption in closing the mental health facility and the telling of my father's tragic story. We hope to inspire public outrage, leading to calls for accountability and change.

The timing was perfect when Jax reached out and made us aware of how unseen things are also aiding our mission to be accomplished. He told us that the Longwells had met up with Blackwell, and once again, they reminded him he was building a house of cards and would be morally bankrupt. They confronted him about his grandchildren's grim future. Jax was shocked to see Blackwood begin to weep. Could it be that he is having a crisis of consciousness?

Dear Bridge Builder, coming to you from the future, I can tell you that it was precisely an inner conflict of his identity, meaning, and purpose. He did, indeed, wonder what his legacy would be.

As Blackwood paced back and forth in the dim light of his office, shadows danced along the walls, mirroring the dissension within his black heart. "*What am I doing?*" he thought, his brow furrowing. He had always cared about his grandkids. Their future and clean air are supposed to be my legacy. Yet he is promoting policies that could destroy their future for his political gain.

He paused, the weight of his thoughts settling on his shoulders. But... industry creates jobs and fuels the economy. Right? People depend on oil and gas for their livelihoods. He thought, "*If I don't play ball, someone else will do it without considering the consequences.*

Isn't it better to be in there as a guiding light and at least mitigate the damage?" All he could do was sigh.

Gazing out the window, he is mindful of the smoke-filled skyline. He harkens back, knowing it is all about power, but it's also about financial stability. He thinks he can be an insider who can push for cleaner fuels in the future while ensuring the energy independence of his Axis of Power, an oil and gas coalition.

He hopes the next generation can still clean up the toxins he has allowed to poison the air and pollute the water. Is that not a rational compromise? The word compromise echoed in his mind like a haunting refrain. But what if he's wrong? What kind of future does he want for his grandchildren? Smoggy air, contaminated rivers, and planet-warming; can he face them, knowing he played a significant role in this setback?

As he imagined their forlorn faces looking up at him, the thought of their dark future saddened him and filled him with guilt. Yet, in his mind, a voice of shame whispered: *"At what cost?"*

He breathed heavily, recalling his many near misses in being brought up on charges and most certainly convicted or, at the least, implicated in some of the most illegal plots that were never revealed. One of the close calls was the land fraud case, in which he and four of his fellow thieves, politicians, knew of future projects and bought land to capitalize on profits.

Eventually, a reporter who caught wind of it was murdered. That was a dark time, and he felt sorry for how far it went. Yet, to sleep at night, he dismissed it as collateral damage.

Attempting to summon peace of mind, Blackwood knew only too well that the road to progress is messy, and yes, compromises are often dirty. The key was to ensure his GOP would come out on the other side with enough influence to steer the narrative toward what he believed. After all, as he reminded his potential partners in clean air crime, drill, drill, drill is a **Three-Billion Dollar Day Industry**! It was essential for him to keep this in focus.

His grandchildren did not need to know every detail. He would win the battles now and protect them later. These random moral dilemmas come with so much pressure. If he falters here, will his grandchildren ever forgive him? He will be firm and lay the groundwork for more gas and oil production, and maybe, someday, they'll understand. Isn't that what every leader must do: sacrifice purity for the greater good?

Once again, he gazed outside, the air still thick with uncertainty. Is it a sacrifice if I plan to ensure the future is better? Or is it merely convenience cloaked in good intentions? Torn between this high-minded philosophy that was surfacing and old-fashioned pragmatism, he couldn't afford to be an idealist in a realist's world. It is time for decisions; the time to act is now. Clenching his jaw strengthened his resolve to take whatever risks lay ahead. He vowed to navigate through whatever choppy waters arose. Wasn't that the actual game of politics?

Blackwood reflects on how he moves strategically through the bustling fundraising events, engaging donors from both sides of the aisle and pickpocketing one group to donate to another — just like he did with the Sherwood project — yet he was no Robin Hood. Politics is not just a forest; it is a threatening jungle where wild beasts, like foreign influences, lie in wait to devour the innocent.

He is both hopeful and wary because he anticipates a mix of support and resistance regarding his plan to have Dick Tador, Presidential nominee, first and foremost dismantle EPA guidelines in favor of pro-oil and gas production. He enlisted Eve and Jax to create a list of pros and cons:

Supportive Responses:

1. Industry Allies: Representatives from energy companies lean in, eager to share their enthusiasm. "This is a smart move," one might say, clapping him on the back. "We need less red tape to innovate and drive growth. The EPA is holding us back from competing on the global stage!"
2. Business Owners: Local entrepreneurs relying on affordable energy sources express gratitude. "Lowering regulations means we can expand our businesses and create jobs. Thank you for standing up for us!"

3. Libertarian Voices: Attendees prioritizing individual freedoms and minimal government intervention cheer him on. "Regulations only stifle our rights! We need leaders willing to challenge the status quo."

Resistance Encounters:

1. Environmental Advocates: Passionate activists at the event speak out, challenging him directly. "Dismantling the EPA guidelines is a dangerous path! We can't sacrifice clean air and water for short-term gains. Our children deserve better!"
2. Moderate Politicians: Members of their party who fear criticism will ask. "Are you sure this is the way to go? The backlash could affect politicians: Constituents might voice their concerns quietly, which will be significant, especially in light of recent climate reports."
3. Public Health Advocates: Doctors and health professionals present could raise alarms. "You need to think about the implications of public health. Higher pollution means higher health-care costs in the long run. Are you prepared for that?"
4. Youth Activists: Young people passionate about climate change approach him, their voices resolute. "You are risking our future! If you dismantle the EPA, you're sending a message that our health isn't a priority. This is a moral issue!"

5. Overall Encounter: As he navigates these discussions, he feels the tension in the air. Pointed questions and critical stares counter-balance each enthusiastic handshake. He knows that maintaining support from diverse groups requires a careful balancing act — he must reassure allies without alienating them. To alleviate his guilt, he will at least bolster the gas and oil's flimsy claim to recycle plastics, and he vows to save the future, just not now.

The Path of Courage

It takes much courage to show your dreams to someone else.

~Erma Bombeck

CHAPTER 50

A rriving at my mother's home, Joy Elisabeth Kincannon, I am welcomed by freshly brewed coffee wafting through her country kitchen and the smell of buttermilk biscuits having been freshly baked. The familiar scents envelop me like a warm embrace.

Sunlight streams through the window, casting a golden glow on the wooden countertops and the quaint decor that has been lovingly curated over the years. I notice her handwritten note, cheerful loops, and swirls reflecting her personality. *"I'll be right back! I just ran to Trader Joe's for fresh strawberries. Help yourself to a cuppa and make yourself at home!"* I pour real cream into my NYC vintage mug, fluff it, and top it off with delicious dark-roasted Peets coffee. Ah, but first, coffee!

With a smile, I wander over to the pantry, where the shelves are lined with jars of homemade preserves and spices, each a testament to my mother's dedication to her craft. The kitchen feels alive with warmth and a sense of nostalgia. I take a moment to admire the rustic details: the open shelves displaying colorful dishes, the farmhouse sink that has seen countless meals prepared, and the well-worn harvest table holding many family gatherings.

With a mug in hand, I settle into a cozy chair by the window, where I can watch the world outside. The garden is vibrant with blooming flowers, and the sweet sound of birdsong fills the air. I cannot help but feel comforted by the familiarity of it all. The love that fills this space is palpable.

I sat in my mother's comfortable and well-appointed home, full of childhood, family, and theatrical photos throughout my brief life. A large studio portrait of my loving and now-deceased great-grandparents hung over the fireplace mantel, gracing the home with their heavenly presence.

I especially appreciated Mom's circle of lifelong friends who frequently traveled together. The pictures of their smiling faces with the alluring backdrops of British Columbia at the Bouchard Gardens, Tulum, Mexico's crystal beaches, and every iconic place imaginable in Greece, France, England, Italy, and, of course, across America continued to fulfill her love of adventure. Her enjoyment of reading and the comfy chairs flanking the fireplace gave me a more profound sense of belonging.

Growing up, there were times when we were more like siblings than mother and son. The blessings of memories and humor raised my spirits. When she returns from the market, I will tell Mom that her keen insights are always welcomed suggestions.

Mom always encouraged me in my acting career, taking me to singing lessons even after working a long and often fatiguing day; she was a trooper. She was never the proverbial stage mom telling me what to do; instead, throughout my years in theatre, she supported me by becoming the youth theatre company's costume organizer.

I was thrilled she was realizing her dreams of traveling. I was also happy to be dog-caring for her chocolate lab, Bruno. This was the perfect opportunity to invest my time in the nearby woods, commune with nature, and take long walks with my pooch pal.

As I sat there, the words and music of a new song began to flow, and the once-before weight of time that had pressed down on me vanished. Music was like that for me; it was therapeutic and creatively fulfilling; it was all the medicine I needed.

Mom returned with much more than strawberries and cooked us a breakfast that even Izzy would have praised. Over another mug of coffee, I told her how much I appreciated everything she had always done for me. I don't say it enough, but I am grateful for you more than I can ever express. You are my biggest cheerleader. Your constant love and encouragement gave me the confidence to pursue my dreams. It is now time for you to live your dreams. You have spent many years caring for me and putting your aspirations aside. It's your time now.

She replied, *"Oh, my dearest Finn, I appreciate that, but I'm just doing what any mother would do. You have brought me so many blessings; seeing you grow into the man you are is incredible. Your work ethic is fantastic, and you have earned everything you've achieved."*

I said, "*No, it's more than that. You have always believed in me, even when I did not think I could achieve that kind of success. Remember when I wanted to start taking acting classes? You worked extra shifts to help pay for them.*"

Mom assured me, "*I knew you were highly talented, and that wasn't through my Mom goggles as everyone could see it. Watching you perform was one of my life's highlights, and I loved every moment. You are an inspiration! Plus, you are deeply passionate, honest, intelligent, imaginative, film-savvy, and your composing skills are uncanny. Son, you are a miracle!*"

Then Mom asked, "*Are you composing anything? I know you have a full plate with work and your studies. Son, I am certain your musical Myrtle Wood will be staged someday. Delays are always blessings in disguise.*"

Since I did not want to worry her, I told her I had some song ideas floating around and was even writing a book. I will surprise her when she returns from her four-month global cruise with the profound project that found me.

"*Mom, on another topic, with the division in today's world, I have been thinking a lot about how people often identify more with their ethnicity or religion than as part of the larger human community,*" I thoughtfully shared.

She understood my propensity to overthink things and replied, "*I know what you mean. It is interesting how deeply rooted those identities can be. Many people's ethnicity and religion shape their values, traditions, and daily lives. This creates a strong sense of belonging, which is essential. However, sometimes, focusing on ethnic or religious identity can divide us rather than unite us. Or it can lead to an "us versus them" mindset.*

People often prioritize their group identity over recognizing our shared humanity. The more we cling to our specific identities, the harder it becomes to connect with others who are different. Finn, this is how it has been since time began. There's much fear involved, too. People frequently feel threatened by people who are different from them, which creates a counterproductive cycle and reinforces those divisions. It's our instinct to want to protect what feels familiar."

I knew what she said was true. Ideally, when we find a balance between our unique backgrounds while recognizing that we are all part of something bigger, we embrace expanding cultural diversity. I was careful not to mention the GOP or WFTP, as the word 'diversity' has become a trigger. It has come at the expense of our shared values as human beings.

Mom said she believed education plays a key role in teaching people about different cultures and beliefs, which fosters understanding and empathy. Learning about each other's stories makes it easier to see the common threads that connect us. Lately, it has also been about respect. We respect our differences while acknowledging that we all want similar things: love, safety, and belonging.

Yes, I agree, as it is about building bridges instead of walls. We should focus more on humanity and create a more inclusive society. It starts with conversations like this — just being willing to talk and listen. Every small step counts. However, the historical carnage of wars that far too many to list have

Mom asked, "Do you want more coffee before my yellow cab arrives to take me to the airport? I have two hours before I must leave."

"Sure, that sounds great!" I added, "Let's play a partial recording of Gawni Grace's historical fiction, Willow Rose, Apothecary. I tapped on my Google Drive and began…

Willow Rose Toussaint

Jesus turned and said to her, "Have courage, daughter.
Your faith has saved you. And the woman was made well."

~Matthew 9:22

CHAPTER 51

My name is Willow Rose Dubois de Toussaint. During my thirty-two years on earth, I have been long aware of the possibility of this horrific moment unfolding. It played out precisely as my ancestors once foresaw; their prophetic visions now befall me.

Some would kill me on this fated night of August 18, 1572. A band of murderous bounty hunters known as Chasseurs de Primes were frantically chasing my infant son Nathaneal through my beloved Dragon Wood. The lucrative reward for my person had attracted ruthless mercenaries, and my only hope was to elude their advances somehow.

My spirit ran as wild as the untamed surroundings, yet this was the only portal to enter the safety of our family catacombs, which would be my redeeming grace. They felt at once far away and then close by. To reach a safe shelter was worth the risk of revealing its magnificent realm's whereabouts. I was blessed in a maniacal twist of fate, knowing that only a person of the purest heart could enter.

With the world's future entrusted to me, outdistancing these brutal hunters was crucial. I pushed myself to keep us moving; you see, not only did my life and destiny hang in the balance, but my three-week-old Nathanael Étienne Toussaint, hidden underneath my flowing emerald-green cloak, securely bound to my breast by a leather sling. He, too, would surely succumb if I were to be slain. My heart was hammering; I ran with all my might to keep us alive.

As the sunlight dimmed, thundering horse hooves pounded the French forest floor, and my pursuers' cursing echoed through the trees — their voices like hounds on my trail. Armed with crossbows and swords, these murderous marauders were a breath's distance behind me. Their partially masked faces could not conceal their evil malice. To escape the grasp of these malicious henchmen, I wove in and out of knolls, groves, and thickets.

The forest loomed before me, tangled with ancient trees and whispering leaves. I darted between the trunks, my breath coming in ragged gasps. The scent of damp earth and moss filled my nostrils, mingling with the sharp tang of fear. I clutched the velvet herb bag at my side; it reminded me of my purpose. Inside were vials of herbs, tinctures, and the remnants of my life as an apothecary — a healer in a world that feared my gifts. I had treated the sick and the wounded, but my wisdom was seen as a threat in these dark times. I had dared to challenge the powerful edicts; now, I was a hunted woman.

The sun dipped low in the sky, casting long shadows that danced across my path. I had memorized the way to my family's catacombs, hidden deep within the forest, a sanctuary carved from stone and secrecy. The predators would be relentless, but I knew these woods better than they did. With each step, I pushed the panic aside, focusing instead on the sounds around me — the rustle of leaves, the distant chirp of crickets, the whisper of the wind. I stumbled upon a narrow path, overgrown and barely visible. It led deeper into the enchanted Dragon Woods, tangled with brambles and thorns, but it was a risk I had to take.

Veering off the main trail, praying the underbrush would hide my scent, I pressed on; the voices behind me grew fainter, swallowed by the thickening night. The forest, a living thing, enveloped me; I even found solace in its depths. I closed my eyes, listening to the earth's heartbeat, the pulse of life that thrummed beneath my feet. I could almost feel the cool touch of the stone walls of the catacombs ahead, the familiar chill that would greet me, and the safety of my ancestors surrounding me. But safety was not guaranteed. The hunters were skilled, and they would not give up easily. With renewed determination, I pressed forward. The moon began to rise, casting silver light through the branches and illuminating my path with a ghostly glow.

Being a respected Apothecary specializing in the blessings, healings, and alchemy of medicinal herbs and roses, the Pope of the Roman Catholic church accused me and hundreds of other healers of heresy, a crime punishable by death. If caught, my fate would be to be drowned, burned at the stake, or hanged from the gallows in the public square, which each had become a spectator sport. Mistakenly accused of being a sorceress, one may ask, just how many witches were executed? None; they were innocent women.

I did not dare to wish my beloved husband Étienne was here for one second. Three hundred and ninety-one kilometers away in Paris, he was safeguarding his longtime friend, King Henry IV, of the majestic Kingdom of Navarre. The king, a Huguenot who was there to marry my childhood friend, Princess Marguerite 'Margot' Valois, a Roman Catholic. Royal weddings, especially this one, would be fraught with turmoil and intrigue.

Escaping the hell-bent goons from my harrowing dilemma was paramount and solely up to me. Immense danger was biting at my heels. Hours ago, what seems like years, when the henchmen attempted to ambush us while I was delivering letters to my neighbors. Their husbands wrote them, who were at my beloved Étienne's side. Thank God I heeded my faithful dog's warning barks, or we would have been trapped. Immediately, I knew what was happening and vowed to be resilient. Fueled by inspiration, we are now miles into the enchanted Dragon Wood.

To keep my long, curly, auburn hair from blowing wildly, I pulled it tight into a chignon and veiled it under my cloak's hood. My sable brown skirt kept snagging on brambles, so I gathered it between my legs, tucked it into the embroidered herb bag's belt, and safely buckled it around my waist. Finally, this arrangement freed us to ride the wind.

I zigzagged through the enchanted Dragon Wood's hidden paths. I am deeply grateful that foraging in this magical forest has given me an uncanny ability to blend into my surroundings seamlessly. Soundlessly, moving through these ancestral grounds, even though the sharp tree branches no longer snag my skirt, they clawed at my face. I would not allow myself to register its excruciating pain. This unexpected endurance assignment was too significant to draw back now. With the wisdom of all ages living within my being, my sole focus was on two things — to survive and, yes, to thrive. The concealed Dejardin catacombs in the heart of the enchanted Dragon

Wood will be our safe harbor until my beloved husband Étienne returns from Paris.

Whether or not the brutal Chaussure brigands knew why they were commissioned to kill me did not matter. They were under the Roman Catholic Pope's strict orders to murder me, or else they would be hanged instead. I would not succumb to feeling exposed or vulnerable to these thugs and their death threats. Instead, I chose to be in harmony with birds of a feather, aligned with my animal totems, and in chorus with the singing trees.

Snapping twigs echoed worryingly through the woods, a chilling reminder that fatal danger was at hand. We were backed into a glen with narrow pathways entrenched by gnarled roots threatening to entrap us. One wrong step could land us in our hired assassins' sight line. After jogging at an even pace and staying close to the tree line, I heard a horse bearing down on us mounted by a brute of a man. Instinctively, I dashed behind a thicket. Alas, being a bit too enthusiastic, I sprinted headlong into bushes whose needle-sharp thorns impaled my body. I felt the intense pain, but I bit my tongue to suppress screaming aloud. Blood dripped from my forehead, yet I could only think of being grateful that my precious baby boy was spared any slashing.

Quickly, I realized weaponizing those needles was possible, even vital. Allowing the predator to get closer to us, I gritted my teeth and grabbed a handful of those razor-sharp thistles, and with all my might, aimed high, pulled tautly, and launched their jagged blades into the axman's bare face. The brutal lashing was so severe that he howled in anguish. His wails spooked his horse, which bucked him into a bramble of briers. The more he fought to be free, the more entangled he became. Ensconced in a prickly predicament, the barbed hook spines yielded the would-be cutthroat to be completely incapacitated. Silently, I cheered and ran as fast as my legs would go!

The dark forest was shrouded in mystery and foreboding. The towering trees loomed overhead, reaching out like skeletal arms toward the sky. The sinister howls and eerie cries of the remaining bounty hunters pierced the silence, sending shivers down my spine... even though unseen creatures moved through the shadows, Nathaneal and I were considered their allies. We could count on them to help us.

The silvery moon's slender strand of light was just enough to make visible a small meadow free of any bounty hunters. When I was about to spirit across its open field, I heard my recently deceased father, Francoise's distinct voice, shouting, "My darling Willow, halt, duck, tuck, and fall down, NOW!"

Instantly, I took heed of this mighty message from 'the beyond.' Folding into an embryonic position, I rolled us atop Mother Earth. Looking up, I noted we had been in the perfect sight, who I would learn was an adept Papal archer. He launched his arrow, which missed us by millimeters; fortunately, it only split the air like an apple into two halves.

Father Francoise prevented the bowman from pinning us to my favorite King Oak tree. As the archer pulled another arrow from his quiver, Father's celestial voice, gently yet firmly, murmured, "Stay Down!" I did not question his command. Obediently, my baby boy and I stayed on the ground in silence. I was especially grateful Nathanael continued to be incredibly quiet.

Puzzled, the bowman looked around, wondering what had happened to his prey. At that exact time, a most fortuitous micro-gust of wind sent his attention elsewhere. He headed toward the distraction and continued following it. Once he was far out of sight, I let loose a long, welcomed exhale and gave good gratitude for my father's supernatural warning.

At my quickest pace, I fought us through the enchanted Dragon Wood, veiled deep within these magical woods was a haven. I wondered if my Aunt Martha would be in our ancestral healing lodge, prepared for this possibility long ago. In unison, I heard my guardian angels, animal totems, ancestors, and ascended experts whispering, "Keep going; we are with you."

With my herb pouch thumping against my hip, I sprinted through the faint glow of the crescent silver moon. I thanked the heavens for the celestial cover of night, a mantle shielding us from our pursuers.

Resting long enough to surveil my enemy, I spied a single huntsman. Concealed in a clutch of shrubbery, he was separated from the others yet vigorously scanning the ground for any sign of my whereabouts. Suddenly, he heard a noise rustling in the trees ahead of me; drawing his bow, he readied himself for a kill shot. At the last minute, he realized it was a deer. His pursuit turned away from us.

As a daughter of the enchanted Dragon Wood, every twist, turn, and embedded stone was etched into the marrow of my bones. Yet, every shadow concealed a potential threat, hinting that the rustle of leaves could be an ambush; I was keen to hear any movement and strained to catch the faintest sound of my pursuers.

With my ancient Apothecial knowledge pulsing through my veins, I barely stayed ahead of these ruthless marauders. However, they were dangerously close, yet I continued to trust in my unseen and seen allies. The symbology of a forest is for life itself.

The huntsmen's flaming torches through the trees cast long, ominous shadows, crafting devilish puppetry to dance upon the underwood. These macabre marionettes were terrifying. Keeping my head on a swivel, I knew this all-but-forgotten part of the world could become our graveyard. I prayed to Jesus, or, as I know him, Yahweh, and my lineage of Myriam, the Magdalena. In an instant, my fast-beating heart was stilled. Asked and answered is a profound promise. Within seconds of my supplication, a miraculous mist mystically whirled, swirled, circled, and surrounded us. To the eyes of the perpetrators, its veil of vapor made my baby boy and me temporarily invisible.

Checking on my sweet son's golden eyes shining up at me, this precious infant had yet to whimper. As a healer, baby Nathaneal intuitively knew the importance of being silent.

I am a Time Traveler and have enmeshed every survival secret in humanity's history within my soul. I thought of Rumi, the 13th-century poet whose mystical words had always spoken to my soul. Taught to me by Aunt Mirelle, the University of Lyon's first female professor, Rumi's poetic prowess inspires me: "I have seen my descent; now watch me rise." Rising above this eerie era of persecution for those with my healing gifts was essential.

There were honest priests in this epochal timeline; there have even been truthful popes, yet not in this chronology. Thankfully, we had moved away from the Roman Catholic Church's horrific Inquisition of the last century, where thousands of people were put to death for being non-Catholics. The presiding Pope Gregory XIII declared its doctrine the ruling religion. However, the Calvinist Reformers, known as French Protestants and called Huguenots, were gaining in numbers. It served these newly minted Christians to worship a God they could connect with without going through a confessional. By the thousands, Aristocrats joined their movement. I was neither, as I was in the commission of Jesus Christ and blessed Myriam of my Magdalena's lineage.

Humbly, I have always experienced extraordinary respect. Because of my family, great favor from the ruling monarchies, and having earned a trustworthy reputation, I am known to be reliable. My precious parents and fabulous aunts never had to remind me how fortunate I was to be alive. Many of my fellow Sojourners were forced and reduced to become rebels, recluses, or societal outcasts.

Contrary to having to go undercover until now, I was sought after by Queens and Kings, nobility and high-born people, priests, and pastors, but not the Pope. Being pursued like wild prey was surreal. My unique lineage, conceived in celestial energy, was born as pure joy to my incredible parents and sanctified by the Magdelena lineage to carry forth the Holy Grail, my destiny.

In 1572, the masses did not know we were here on earth to create, cultivate, and relish beauty, bliss, and blessings, to savor the earth's goodness and heaven's grace. Are we not the manifestations of the Creator, beloved children of God? Our extraordinary mission is to elevate, elucidate, and evolve humanity through luminous divine love, sublime light, and forgiveness, not by religion but by spirit. In this overly challenging, chaotic, and collective wheel of time, I am here to heal not just bodies but hearts and souls. The mission is to break the ironclad chains of war, famine, fear, and death's cyclic patterns.

Having been to the future, I knew this War of Religion would last over thirty-eight years; this was only year twelve. Terror gripped

293

the hearts of both Huguenots and Roman Catholics. It is time to change history and save the future.

Pausing only a minute to relieve the gasping wheezes of my breath, thoughts of the flower-filled sanctuary known as Sacred Rose Herbarium filled my heart. I dared not think I may ever see it or my family again. Instead, I allowed these revered images to bless me. From age to age, Sacred Rose was where our ancestors called home. I continued to drink in this energy elixir, which anointed my soul with the courage to keep going. Gathering us up for another run towards the catacombs in the protection of night was wise.

Suddenly, in the depths of the enchanted Dragon Wood, the sheltered silence was shattered by the footsteps of those who would kill us. I felt the henchmen's dark energy, tangible even in the dense foliage. Dashing us through a thicket of undergrowth whose overhead canopy was impenetrable so that only slivers of moonlight could patch its way through, my heart began to pound again. From within our forested laird, I could see the bounty hunters moving swiftly towards us. Malevolence silhouetted their oaf-like bodies; they resembled ghostly grim reapers whose evil eyes of fixed fortitude could cut through trees.

With each passing moment, the chase was a deadly game of cat and mouse, where any misstep could mean the end of our lives. They were tracking us unremittingly with calculated precision, so imagine my relief when an errant noise sent these murderers careening in another direction. I loped again toward the catacombs despite my heavy breathing. Hope was not lost. I pushed past old limitations by weaving through the trees and bounding over fallen logs — my determination to evade capture burned brightly from within. Driven, despite exhaustion and encouraged by the crescent moon hanging high in the sky, it cast an ethereal glow over the enchanted Dragon Wood.

However, the heavy footfalls that echoed through the quiet forest announced the bounty hunters' return. At that very moment, I heard flowing water coming from behind a boulder; looking around, I was ecstatic to discover a glistening waterfall. I had never known its existence; desperation powered my sprint toward its magical cascade.

At best, I hoped to use its melodic noise as a cover. With my last burst of energy, I leaped onto the embankment and slid behind the waterfall, whose water curtain shielded us from sight. Listening attentively, hearing the heartless hunters pass us by, their footsteps faded into the distance. I sighed with deep relief.

I took this opportunity to rest and ponder how magnificent life truly is. With the serendipitous surprise of a waterfall brooking over a stream, synchronicity washed over me. The forest is a powerful metaphor for life; its vast and intricate paths represent our choices. Within their depths, stories come alive, weaving narratives that inspire us to trust the process of existence. Just as the forest is filled with shadows and light, life encompasses joys, sorrows, challenges, and championships, teaching us that strength arises from adversity.

In fairy tales, we encounter characters who venture into the unknown, much like in our lives. The brave knights, clever maidens, and wise creatures navigate through trials that mirror our struggles. We may face dark forests filled with uncertainty, yet we emerge transformed. These stories remind us that the journey is as important as the destination, as growth often occurs in the most unexpected places. The magic of the forest resonates with our archetypal selves, tapping into deep-seated truths about human experience. It invites us to explore our fears and dreams, confront the monsters that lurk in the shadows, and seek the light that breaks through the canopy.

Just as the forest is alive with whispers of ancient wisdom, so are our lives enriched by the lessons we glean from the stories we tell and the experiences we endure. Every twist and turn in the forest serves as a reminder that life is not a straight path, but a winding journey filled with revelations. It teaches us patience, encouraging us to pause and appreciate the beauty around us, even in moments of hardship. Like life, the forest thrives on growth, decay, and renewal cycles, illustrating that endings are often the seeds of new beginnings.

We are asked to believe in our inner strength and embrace the magic within us. The fairy tales we cherish echo these truths, guiding us through the labyrinth of existence and helping us recognize that, like the forest, we are a complex and beautiful creation. In this way, the forest becomes a sanctuary of wisdom, reflecting the intricate dance of life. Once, there was no sound from our pursuers. I stepped back into the woods and continued to flee. Being fleet of foot, courage became a guiding light to navigate the darkness and uncertainty.

Thanking the Creator, I am only minutes away from our ancestral catacombs. Once safely inside and rested, I will write love letters to my beloved Étienne and our precious six-year-old twins, Abigaelle Orianne and Gabrielle Suzanne, who are being educated in the Kingdom of Navarre's storybook castle. My beautiful mother, Maryse de Jardin Dubois, attends to their wishes.

Thinking of my father, the late Professor Francoise DuBois's supernatural help, I am grateful to have inherited his renowned intuition, gifts of time travel, and healing abilities. The irony was not lost on me that these are the very reasons why I have become a source of great angst to the Catholic Church. They fear that I am a rival to their power, and they would be correct. I stand for divine love, not misbeliefs.

Willow Rose
Apothocary

Sharyn G. Jordan
Storyteller

Sacred Catacombs

Divine in its glory is the hearth's bright glow
Passionately, she burns brightly the matters of heart
'Tis the Soul's sacred fire that keeps lit our destiny.

~ Sharyn G. Jordan

CHAPTER 52

S eeking refuge in my family's catacombs, a hidden sanctuary beneath the city's bustling streets, we have arrived at the secret portal concealed by foliage and moss. Lifting the heavy wooden door with the lever designed just for me, should I ever enter from this vantage, the pulley still worked as it had in past years.

Before closing the door, I secured the living concealments. Upon entering the inner sanctums, the blessings of Ada, the name of our vaults, surrounded me. Ada is a living entity whose Hebrew origins mean 'adornment.' In her eerie stillness, she proves to be a deeply appreciated reprieve. As the sun rises higher in the sky, light is cast into the cavernous tunnels below. Stepping inside the foyer, it is still a bit dark. I found the stained-glass lantern on the shelf just inside the earthen sanctuary. I struck the waiting flint against the steel patch, producing the perfect spark to be caught on the charcloth, and transferred it to the tinder box.

The handle was at hand, and the striker was affixed to it. Navigating the lantern-lit passageways lined with ancient relics and jars of potent herbs of my expertise in crafting potions and remedies, I brushed away cobwebs. From there on in, it is a bit tricky as turning around in the tunnel's early stage was purposely tight. Once I found my footing, I remembered to count exactly eleven paces. I felt for a hidden doorway whose handle, with just the right touch, swiveled open on a single pivot.

Descending below, stepping onto every narrow platform of the steep stairway, I counted one, two, three... to twenty-two, which took us lower into the catacomb's belly until I arrived at a wide dais. Another count of thirty-three paces landed us at the ancient sanctuary's portal. Although my Aunts Monet and Mirelle were in Paris attending the royal wedding of King Henry IV and Marguerite de Valois, my heart quickened with the anticipation of seeing my Aunt Martha.

To alert my mother's oldest sister, Martha, Keeper of the sacred caves, of our presence, I pulled down the strong cord of the interior chimes. I could hear the bell's peal ripple through the tunnels to the main living space. Since we were far below the surface, no one above ground could listen to their melodic ringtones.

Finally, I am hidden from prying eyes and know that venturing outside can mean capture or worse for us. My resolve to survive and protect our family's legacy drives me to continue my resourcefulness and resilience. Even though they were tested, I am reminded to rely on my wit, intuition, and wisdom of the healing arts to outsmart those who seek to harm us in the shadows.

This knowledge of healing arts helps me find solace in the generations of my family and draw strength from ancestral spirits who once walked these hallowed halls. Despite the constant danger and uncertainty, I am discovering a hidden strength within myself— a toughness that allows me to endure. Eventually, I will emerge from the shadows as a symbol of courage and defiance against tyranny. Our secret caves were known only to our family.

Gently, I unbound Baby Nathaniel, sat us on the oversized ruby-red divan, and nursed my remarkable infant son. I was in awe of his penchant for endurance; down to my bones, his trust strengthened me. Our harrowing experience would forge our enduring, lifelong, deep bond. Once he was sound asleep, I replenished my spent energy on delicious bread, crisp apples, and dried meats. I counted the blessings of my precious Aunt Martha, who stocked the pantries well. While drifting off to sleep, gratitude filled my heart.

As I slept, the history of the sacred catacombs played itself as a dream going back to when it was first acquired. These celestial caves, mysteriously residing beneath the earth since before time began, are a testament to our persistent heritage. Skilled family members and artisans have refined the walls, improved upon the hall of majesty, and luxuriously paved the corridors with gemstones. This has been our Holy Order's hallowed haven for five and half centuries, a living embodiment of our legacy. Its rustic elegance beholds the energy of divine love. Our exquisite Ada, with her bejeweled-hued satin and velvet fabrics, lavishly drapes the clay walls and transports me to faraway lands and the inner kingdom of my BEing. Gracing the stately main room are four topaz-colored, comfortable chairs set upon lovely oriental rugs from my father's friends from the Orient; they covered the hard-packed dirt floors.

Our harvest tablescape is an altar of beeswax candles and vases of fresh wildflowers. In the bedroom, a wistful bed stuffed with our goose-down feathers refreshed the weariest of souls. The anticipation of a bath and the comfort of being lusciously covered with family heirloom quilts and silk throws, sewn in love by our Lyonnaise craft ladies, brought a sense of warmth and security.

Central to the main room is a low-slung oak table in the round, with hand-woven baskets overflowing with paper for sketching, journaling, and writing. First established in Lyon in 1472, a local printer began publishing French, Greek, Latin, Italian, Hebrew, and Spanish books. Since the Catholic regime in Rome had held Parisian printers to strict guidelines, Lyon quickly became prominent in the European publishing revolution. This rich history fills me with pride; considering all my liberties, I am fortunate to have been born in luminous Lyon.

A book I assisted in authoring by our family friend and my godfather, Nostradamus, a visionary and an apothecary, contained potions, in-depth astrological calculations, and his eight hundred quatrains. These tomes were written when the governing patriarchy was creating apocalyptic expectations. A brutal era barely lifted above the lowest of common denominators. Nostradamus wielded a powerful influence over the Queen Mother, Catherine de Medici. It was my Apothecarial knowledge that summoned me to her Parisian palace. In Nostradamus' 1555 Almanac, he referenced my visionary abilities and our time travel talents. Catharine was curious, and the Pope was furious.

Indeed, life holds ongoing learning opportunities. The blessings of growing up with these and additional luminaries taught me the joys of thinking and living in freedom. To not outsource my spiritual life to religiosity, my studies proved how history's long drama continually played itself out through the papacy, problems, power, and public disorder. Wash, rinse, and repeat until the cycle changes, yet it stays the same for the masses forever.

For those who divinely dwell in Magdalena & Yeshua, Christ's unconditional love, this life is filled with beauty, grace, and gratitude.

Thankfully, daylight's brightness streams through the intentional overhead openings not seen from the above forested floor. These carefully placed forest floor areas are well disguised and sealed with opaque resin, allowing natural light to illuminate our underground dwelling. I feel Father, Mother, and God's essence of pure peace. It is palpable. We stand in the glow of a radiant sun, bathing us in divine light. I give thanks for having safely arrived.

Returning to the 21st Century, Mom and I were inspired by Willow's challenges. Her yellow cab arrived. I carried out her luggage, embracing her; I said, "I love you, Mom."

ARTIST VS. ACTIVIST

Artists are the gatekeepers of truth.
We are civilization's radical voice.

~Paul Robeson

CHAPTER 53

Dearest Bridge Builder,

h ave you ever heard of one of my heroes, Paul Robeson? He was an activist, attorney, all-American football player, actor, and beloved singer who spoke out for civil rights and faced political controversy — a victim of McCarthyism. In Lucas films, per *The Young Indiana Jones Adventures*, the 2007 documentary on Paul will break your heart. His son shares that his brilliant father was brush-stroked by history when he asked whether it was more important to be an artist or a prophet. He replied, "an artist."

Grappling with the weight of my information and the dangerous consequences of revealing it, I am navigating a perilous labyrinth of lies, corruption, cover-ups, and a treacherous web woven from deceit. In a pulse-pounding race against time to expose the truth, preserve our future, and positively change history, I am using every ounce of my energy, courage, and resourcefulness to outwit these menacing adversaries.

With the themes of corruption and power, this letter to you, and hopefully, I'll live long enough to complete my novel to the best of my ability. It examines how power can corrupt, and the lengths megalomaniacs will go to maintain control. I am learning to embrace the ongoing struggle between self-preservation and the responsibility to speak out against injustice, which is a balancing act. Izzy's, Willow's, and my overarching message emphasizes the importance of fighting for a better future despite overwhelming odds.

This was a monster story of grand proportions! Evolving my self-doubt into becoming a catalyst of change was beyond transformational. Transitioning from an animated Fine Arts student to a whistleblower was tumultuous, yet it galvanized my commitment to creating a future world of sustainable energy, clean air, empathy, kindness, and peace.

Prioritizing my time was essential; juggling classes, my part-time work, and my art projects was increasingly challenging. Since my days were filled with lectures, studio time, and shifts at the posh country club, it left little room for rest. Late nights sifting through documents and gathering evidence of newfound knowledge profoundly affected my psyche and lifestyle. Thankfully, the urgency to expose the truth overshadows my commitment to serve.

The political corruption I uncovered was a mental barrier to creativity. Once overflowing with ideas and inspiration, writing or composing is difficult for me. The art that once served me as an outlet now feels trivial compared to the demanding need to expose the truth. The emotional turmoil manifests as a creative block, leaving me frustrated and anxious.

As the pressure mounts, my relationships with friends and fellow artists strain — the fear of implicating them in dangerous political corruption leads to isolation. Friends notice my withdrawal and increased anxiety. Struggling to articulate the gravity of the situation, I fear they will dismiss the imperativeness of the threat.

The expectation and necessity to maintain passing grades become more difficult as I devote time to our investigation. The terror of failing looms large as my scholarships hinge on academic performance. The thought of disappointing my family and losing the opportunity to make a difference in the world, I ask myself, what is the value of my creativity if the world and I are falling apart? This internal conflict between an artist and an activist creates a profound disconnection.

What would you say to someone who argues that Tador, whose rhetoric is vile and offensive, mentored by the very people who imposed McCarthyism, is being placed in a position of leadership makes sense? I say, It does not.

My motivations in combating corruption may be my demise; however, I will have at least sounded the alarm to the death of democracy as we once knew it. We must stay grounded and be vigilant when everything around us falls apart. I am working on that.

Our liberties are lessons from the past and remind us of the importance of nurturing democratic values and ensuring that the voices of all citizens are amplified. By striving for inclusivity and fairness, societies can mitigate the risk of conflict and work towards a future where the hard-won freedoms of the present are preserved and celebrated. Ultimately, the historical patterns we observe are not merely reminders of past struggles but also serve as guides for navigating future challenges. In its vastness, the universe embodies a fundamental truth: pursuing justice and freedom is a timeless journey that requires constant vigilance and active participation from all.

Victory Abounds

It is better to concur yourself than to win a thousand battles. Then the victory is yours. It cannot be taken from you, not by angels or demons, heaven or hell.

~Buddha

CHAPTER 54

When Izzy and Sheamus arrived at my Mom's to commemorate Genesis's impressive election lead, Izzy served us a red, white, and blue banana split whipped with real cream. Strawberries and blueberries piled atop three scoops of vanilla ice cream drizzled with chocolate syrup. It was divine.

We were also celebrating my progress in writing *The Kincannon Legacy*, but much to their surprise, the unveiling of my grandmother Gawni's historical fiction book was also on our agenda. This trifecta was a redeeming place in time. With all we have been through together, we three very different people have grown incredibly close in just a short time.

We are thrilled as we watch the television's evidence of Genesis being in the lead. The extent to which we have revealed the levels of corruption that continue to surface is rewarding. The dismantling of the EPA, blatant disinformation, and low-level behavior that tried to hijack our future was our foreign enemies' goal. For decades, they have attempted to transition our beautiful country into an authoritarian, autocratic nation. But no, not on our watch!

We hoped Genesis would call for an FBI probe into their blatant interference with the elections through social media deception. To launch an investigation into the crooked politicians, their bullying, bashing, lying, and money laundering on both sides of the aisle was mandatory.

As the results were rolling in, I shared the audio I had played for my Mom with Izzy and Shaemus as it reflected the synchronicity of how we are also threading a tapestry with a more profound sense of connection to the past and a renewed appreciation for the sacrifices and bravery of all those who have gone before us. Willow is the remarkable story of Izzy and my magnificent medieval ancestor, exemplified heroism immortalized in this noble novel's pages, filled us with a profound sense of gratitude.

Bringing this incredible story to life, saving it from obscurity, and ensuring that it will be passed down to future generations is a legacy. Willow's story of saving the future will inspire and captivate readers for years. This trilogy, Book One, is published in the Chinese Yang Wood Dragon year. For Gawni Grace's treasured project, this is the perfect time.

My grandmother, Grace, was named after her 16th-century ancestor, Grace O'Malley, a legendary Irish chieftain. The name translates to joy, beauty, goodness, generosity, strength, and resilience, as well as one who possesses the pearls of wisdom.

She is well-versed in ancient folklore. Since she began reading to me when I was a baby, it may well be one of the reasons I have become an accomplished composer, actor, and poet. Storytelling continues to enrich me. As an esteemed Elder of the Sacred Imaginist Circle, Gawni decodes the mysteries, magic, and miracles of the mystical Wheel of Time.

The connection of her historical fiction tells precisely where Tador's platform and political pundits wanted to take us back to medieval times. Set in sinister synchronicity, it begins in the horrific era of women accused of being heretics by a jealous church. The Pope decreed these gifted apothecaries' blessings, prayers, and healings unholy. He went to great lengths to strip the sacred, sanctifications, and sacraments that Jesus brought to earth. Sacrificing his body, blood, and bones on Calvary, the Hill of Golgotha, Christ's mission was for us to be in direct contact with the Creator.

When the apostle Peter preferred that Jesus behave as a worldly King of the Jews, like a wealthy Roman emperor, he was furious that instead, Jesus was a hippie. Love, peace, and harmony were his message.

When Peter began the Catholic church after the crucifixion, it was patterned after the pomp and circumstance of the nobility.

By the 12th century, the church was selling "Get Out Of Hell Free" cards called Indulgences. The first known use of plenary indulgences was in 1095 A.D. when Pope Urban II remitted all penance of persons who participated in the crusades and confessed their sins. Later, indulgences were also offered to those who couldn't go on the Crusades but offered cash contributions to the effort instead. This is one of the sources of the church's inordinate wealth. It is part of a grander story that Willow champions. It is the heart of Martin Luther's edicts to the church and is the beginning of Protestantism.

We love our Mother Mary, Myriam, the Magdalena and Jesus the Christ's mystical teachings, and evidence of His miracles. Interestingly enough, the premise of priests, preachers, and popes was unnecessarily installed by Constantine to intercede on our behalf.

Willow grew up with the more profound truth of Jesus and Magdalena's divine love, yet she faced resistance from powerful forces intent on preserving the status quo. The church created misinformation that Myriam, Mary Magdalene, was a prostitute to discredit her and suppress her transformative message. Her archetypal methodology dates from time immortal and sheds light on a profoundly intimate connection between Magdelene and Jesus.

Their quest for humanity resonates with themes of salvation and liberation across time and space. Willow Rose was privy to the secrets of this ancient truth, a narrative that challenges conventional beliefs and offers a radical perspective. Willow's luminous love letters unveil how Myriam, the Magdelena, and Jesus the Christ advocated for human dignity, equality, and spiritual freedom. Their shared mission challenged oppressive systems and empowered individuals to seek redemption beyond conventional constraints and to be directly connected to the Creator. They taught us that the Kingdom is within.

Myriam the Magdelena is a key figure in Jesus' inner circle, yet there was an ongoing conspiracy to undermine her role as a spiritual leader. With Jesus, she was a peaceful activist, a powerful voice for the marginalized, oppressed, and disenfranchised. Their known intimacy was far too liberal for the minds of the day, especially given the partial story the church was telling of Jesus the Christ. It better fits the clergy's narrow narrative, supporting the stripping away of the unconditional love and supernatural gifts that Jesus himself came to give us. It has created a series of 'us against them' scenarios of false judgments. When, in fact, the joy, exaltation, and ecstasy of Jesus and Myriam are exquisite

The Kingdom of God is a profound concept that transcends and represents a state of being where individuals live in alignment with the principles of compassion, justice, and unity. In Jesus' teachings, the Kingdom of God is not merely a distant realm or a future promise; instead, it is an invitation to recognize and cultivate the presence of the divine in the here and now. It signifies an evolutionary experience where the heart is open to love, and relationships are grounded in understanding and respect. In this kingdom, barriers that separate people dissolve, and communities flourish through mutual support and shared values.

It is characterized by a sense of belonging, where everyone is welcomed and valued regardless of their background or beliefs. It teaches that true fulfillment comes not from material possessions or societal status but from serving others and nurturing the spirit of generosity. It encourages us to embrace the divine within ourselves and others. His teachings emphasize that everyone is capable of transformation.

Willow, Jesus, and Mary Magdalene are a testament to the power of love and its ability to transcend boundaries. It reminds us that we are all part of a grand story that is continually being written as we navigate the complexities of life. The lineage of love is alive within us. As Jesus promised,

"Truly, truly, I say to you, whoever believes in me will also do the works that I do; and greater works than these will he do because I am going to the Father." ~ John 14:12.

During our celebration, Agent Agatha Christi called to warn me that my file had been opened without authorization. Telling me to watch my back; if I were to be followed, it would not be from her.

Shaemus was concerned about this turn of events. Regardless of the election's results, if Blackwood had a mole at the FBI, there would surely be retaliation. He then told Izzy and me about something he had wanted to share for weeks. It was a bombshell: Agent Agatha Christi and Eve Everhart are sisters.

Well, of course, that makes total sense. I told them of when I saw Eve coming to the diner to see Agatha and how intense their conversation had been.

Shaemus explained that they were indeed their daddy's precious girls, and when Jake Burnett was killed, they both knew he had been murdered. Eve is also Agatha's CSI. They have been building a case against Blackwood, who was on the Obsidian Board of Directors for ten years. Sadly, just like President John F. Kennedy's assassination over his intentions of pulling out of Vietnam, their dad's death for wanting to be in green energy will probably never be solved.

It was time for us to call it a night, and oh, what a night it was. As we joined hands, radiant energy surrounded us, merging our joys, gratitude, and love into a collective force that vibrates with pure light. This convergence is a powerful reminder that we have not been alone in pursuing joy and connection.

In this moment of unity, we understand that they are part of something greater than themselves, a movement of love that transcends time and space. Izzy and Shaemus then left on a high note. We promised to meet for coffee at Oakwood to hail President Genesis's victory. We were elated!

Oh, My God!
What Happened?

There are three kinds of people in this world:
people who make it happen, people who watch what
happens, and people who wonder what happened.

~Tommy Lasorda

Chapter 55

On a high note, Izzy and Shaemus said good night. We promised to meet for coffee at Oakwood to hail President Genesis's victory. We were elated! Before going to bed, I tapped my phone off. It was the first time I had done so since this entire tangled web of mystery was unveiled. After a great night's rest, I was exhilarated to awaken with a sense of accomplishment.

Bruno was ready to go for a walk, so I kept my phone, turned off, and basked in the glow of victory. It was the best walk ever! Returning my pooch pal to Mom's backyard, I drove to Oakwood. Turning my car's CD player to its highest volume, I belted out a song from John Water's musical, Hairspray, *"You Can't Stop The Beat."* I was beyond thrilled.

Arriving at Izzy's private office, tears were streaming down her cheek. It gutted me; what on earth could have happened? She said, "Oh, Finn, I cannot believe that Dick Tador won the Electoral Votes and is our president. Yes, the fix was in." Oh, My God!!

Dearest Bridge Builder,

The following months felt like a hazy daze. It was inconceivable that Genesis was not our commander-in-chief and that an unqualified man, a puppet, pawn, and jester, would be at the helm.

On the day of the inauguration, I felt a pit in my stomach as large as a boulder. I couldn't bear to watch Dick Tador being sworn in with his billionaire band of thieves sitting on the dais right behind him. Blackwood was grinning from ear to ear as if he had just pulled off the biggest heist of his political career. And indeed, from all appearances, he had. Yet, as we know, things are never as they seem.

The song "A Whiter Shade of Pale" by Procol Harem began playing in my head. It was a 1967 anthem when peace, love, and harmony were paramount. Indeed, we 'tripped the light fandango,' and just like its mystical ballad, we got f***ed.

Echoes of history resonated within me, a reminder that the fight for truth is as old as civilization itself. I could have been your better advocate. With your future in my heart, I pray my experiences reveal the truth behind the corruption that seeped into our government's blood and crept into its bones like cancer. Here we are, connected to ongoing patterns in which the ties that bind still hold us hostage.

The dark web will stop at nothing to protect their secrets; therefore, I write not as a coward but as a man who refuses to be silenced. As I have shared, if you are reading this book, I have succumbed to the shadows that have relentlessly pursued me. I believe my sacrifice will not be in vain.

To prevent my proof from disappearing, I have securely hidden Blackwood recordings, dates, and the names of his co-conspirators in a safety deposit box. A trusted colleague knows the bank where I stashed the evidence files labeled with code names and encrypted messages that unravel the web of deceit.

With every revelation, I have become more determined to fight for transparency and bring down those who seek to undermine our country's democratic foundation. As I dig deeper into the conspiracy, I continue to uncover shocking secrets and face threats from all sides; an unwavering belief in the power of truth and justice fuels me. I am willing to risk everything to ensure the corrupt plot is brought to light and democracy is preserved.

The legacy of human and spiritual rights becomes a battleground of ideologies, and just like Willow Rose, I, too, am caught in the crossfire of competing narratives. The truth is waiting to expose the rot at the heart of our nation. If you dare to pursue justice, follow the trail I have left behind. You will find a network of betrayal. If I fail, you can pick up where I left off. I encourage you to take up this mantle, act upon your moral obligation, and create a more empathic world one person at a time.

May your life unfold as my grandmother Gawni taught me: in peregrination. It is a Celtic homage to life, which is a blessed journey, a profound pilgrimage of time, and an ongoing, spiraling prayer. 'Tis a sacred process: attuning to gratitude and being open-hearted.

I Am Sorry.
Thank You.
Forgive Me.
I Love You.

~Ancient Ho'oponopono Prayer

And my life has forever changed. This is my story. May God bless you.

True to my commitment, I wrote a graphic tell-all novel. After crafting the satirical theme, I was especially aware of its surrealism. *The Kincannon Legacy, Last Will, and Testament* is a robust account of controversial conversations between power brokers I overheard at a clandestine dinner party hosted by Senator Blackwood.

Ever since that event and especially after the horrid inauguration, my dreams or, instead, nightmares have been of an impending dystopia.

Pouring my thoughts into every word I type may be my only legacy; I must express my deeply held values and experiences. As a victim of childhood bullying, eating disorders, depression, and fear resulted from those experiences. However, through Myrtle Wood Clinic's therapy, I was able to foster a deep sense of worthiness within my being. I learned to stand firm against organized intimidation, discrimination, and dehumanization. It became my life lesson, inspiring me to embark on a transformational journey for myself and my loved ones. Those adversities now serve me.

Having written my book that intertwines esoteric knowledge with practical application, invites Bridge Builders on a journey where ancient wisdom is a guiding light in today's fast-paced world. It offers the opportunity to delve deep into timeless truths, encouraging personal growth and self-discovery while addressing contemporary challenges. By blending profound insights with actionable strategies, our narrative envisions a more peaceful and harmonious existence.

As each page unfolds, it encourages us to explore our inner landscape, fostering a connection between the mystical and the mundane, ultimately revealing the path to a transformed inner and outer world.

It culminates with the truth that worn-out and detrimental patterns will repeat until they are changed. Indeed, we are the catalysts of Beauty, Apothecaries, Alchemists, Bridge Builders, and the Phoenix. In these epochal times of evolution, we will rebuild, renew, and rise above. Let us reset, never regret; refine, and recalibrate systems; lean into individual and collective gratitude to cultivate and create an ineffable, inclusive, and inspirational future. Thank you.

Blessings,
Finn

WHERE DISRUPTIA DWELLS

My world is fire and blood.
As it fell, each of us, in our own way, was broken.

~Mad Max, "Fury Road"

CHAPTER 56

Dark dreams interrupted my once-upon-a-time solid night's sleep. Visions of a dystopian world called *Disruptia* was a tapestry of neon lights and looming shadows. The sky was a perpetual shade of gray, a testament to the thick pollution over the cities. Corporations ruled the land, their influence seeping into every crevice of daily life. Privacy was a distant memory; citizens moved like robots via a world order that watched their actions. It would be a time when government-controlled news channels contrived fear, control, and disinformation. Artificial Intelligence ran legislative agencies, usurped human creativity, and diminished the realms of imagination.

I had always been a dreamer, a boy who looked up at the stars and wondered what lay beyond. However, years earlier, stumbling upon something sinister, I recall asking if these images were premonitions. True to Agent Agatha Christi Collin's warning, I was constantly followed by devious men whom Izzy and I called the Shadow People.

Plus, the Emperor — the same man Izzy saw in her clairvoyance months ago — had finally shown himself. We nicknamed him Lucifer Laciferous; he was the prominent leader of the Cabal with an extreme agenda. Although he was not nominated or voted in by "We the People," he would be the land's most significant and utmost power broker.

Ironically, once Dick Tador took office, Blackwood was thrown under the bus, proving there is there no honor among thieves. Yet, his Oil and Gas Project was a huge success: the EPA was dismantled.

Dick Tador's anti-climate change policies were but a thin veil for an ambitious authoritarian regime. Hidden in bureaucratic jargon and coded language, my dreamscape caped crusader knew this would strip people of their freedoms and actions and manipulate lives through technology. But telling people was another matter. The fear of being silenced loomed over me, both in my nightmares and in real life.

I, too, was becoming much more fragile. To alleviate my griev-
ing, depression, and swirling mood swings, I sought out a psychia-
trist named Dr. Daniel Elijah Solomon, who prescribed a series of
medical cocktails. However, my mind was far too delicate to process
these synthetics. I spiraled farther out of reality. Since I was seeking
solace, I even resorted to self-medicating with alcohol. It numbed the
pain and would temporarily cease the agony. I was often reminded
of my dad's hero, David, and of the many fallen soldiers who our
government murdered in the name of profit.

To bolster my faith, I studied religions, and perhaps because of
it, I had vivid Irish dreams. Dating back to St. Patrick's time in the
magical Emerald Isle, he had difficulty converting the Celts to Roman
Catholicism. They were happily steeped in their beautiful traditions,
spirituality, and pantheon deities. For instance, their patron saint of
Ireland, the abbess St. Brigid, was an adored goddess of fire, a poet,
and a blessed healer. Pope Celestine I, 5th Century, instructed Patrick
to retell the sacred Winter Solstice and spiritual Spring Equinox
stories from a Christian point of view. Since nowhere in the Bible
are dates for this immaculately conceived birth of our Lord and his
crucifixion given, over time, it was successfully installed. Both can
live in harmony.

My dreams took me to the depths of winter, where I felt the
chill of its solstice. In this time of darkness, it was added that this was
the birth of our baby Jesus. I witnessed the love and joy that came
with celebrating his holy birth. Families gathered in the flickering
light of candles, sharing stories of hope and renewal as they awaited
the return of longer days. The cold nights were filled with laughter
and love as they kept the fire of faith burning bright against the
winter's grasp.

The Celts celebrated the Spring Equinox's Goddess Ostara,
representing the dawn, spring season, and fertility. It is a time of
rebirth and renewal. The Pope declared a new significance to the
Christian calendar; our Celtic spring equinox was now associated
with Christ's crucifixion of Jesus. It was a moment of sacrifice and
redemption, remembering the trials faced by the savior as they

embraced the warmth of the sun returning. It became the Christian Holy Days for Easter.

In my lush dreamscapes, I found myself captivated by these distant pasts. As I drifted into slumber each night, visions of the Celtic and St. Patrick's Ireland unfolded. I saw the abundant fields and blossoming flowers and felt ancient stone structures' magic and sacredness. The vibrant celebrations of sacred beliefs surrounded me. In these dreams, I experienced a world where the welcoming of spring and the arrival of winter were not just seasonal changes but significant moments of spiritual birth and rebirth. Honoring Easter, Christmas, St. Brigid, and Ostara are times of joy.

I witnessed gatherings of beautiful villagers, their faces illuminated by the glow of bonfires, singing hymns that echoed through the valleys. They honored the equinox, a time of balance between light and dark, reflecting on life's and death's mysteries. As I wandered through my utopia, I felt the weight of history and the intertwining of faith and nature.

Through these dreams, I began to understand the profound connection between nature's cycles and my faith's teachings. I saw how the earth's rhythms mirrored the story of salvation, weaving together the themes of death and rebirth, darkness and light. Each season held its significance, inviting reflection and reverence.

I was determined to warn others of a society careened toward the future I had foreseen. I felt the weight of anticipation mixed with dread in my dreamscape. The streets were quieter than usual, a tense silence settling over the city as the night deepened. I had to take one last stand to ensure our message reached as many people as possible.

I devised a plan and gathered Izzy, Sheamus, and Jax together as we still believed in freedom. But where was Shaemus? We could not reach him; his phone had gone silent. I sent Agent Agatha Christi to check on him, but he was nowhere to be found. Everything was intact in his home, with no sign of struggle. Yet, it was as if he had vanished off the face of the earth.

Jax, Izzy, and I met in an old library's crumbling crypt. The historical registry's stately upper floors numbered in the teens and overflowed with books, maps, museum treasures, and ancient scrolls.

Yet, the basement's air was thick with dust, and the scent of forgotten stories was evident. Each meeting was a risk, but the flicker of hope ignited within us was worth it.

We pieced together a network of those who still held on to the compassion of our humanity. I knew that to reach the masses, we needed a method that could not be quickly silenced. I turned to the underground art community, vibrant painters, poets, storytellers, and musicians who railed against the new regime like us.

With their help, we created a series of murals of joy, sacred spoken word performances, and poetry that was a medicine that told the timeless tales of our beloved nation. Each piece was a call to awareness, a plea to resist the impending doom and to speak up.

In my recurring dreams, the government began cracking down on dissidents. Reminiscent of Fascism, Anti-Semitism, Communism, Socialism, and tyrannical Monarchies were being played out. Books such as George Orwell's *1984*, Aldous Huxley's *Brave New World,* Ray Bradbury's Fahrenheit 451, and Margaret Atwood's *The Handmaiden's Tale* were trying to come true. However, our collective voices were strong.

Would the time come when surveillance drones patrolled the streets, and anyone caught speaking against Dick Tador's government was swiftly dealt with? Thankfully, the freedom seeds of rebellion had already been sown. The murals spread like wildfire, and warnings circulated through the city.

We gathered for one final meeting in the library basement; everyone's beautiful faces were illuminated by candlelight. We discussed our next steps, but as we spoke, a loud crash echoed from above, followed by the heavy thud of boots on the stairs. The regime had caught wind of our activities. Panic surged through the room as the door burst open, revealing armed Shadow Men clad in dark uniforms. My heart pounded as our situation became transparent. Izzy and Jax scattered, but I stood frozen for a moment, torn between escape and the urgency of our message. I could not let our sacrifice be in vain.

The Shadow Men accosted and handcuffed me; something cracked my head wide open, all the way to my scalp; blood flowed like a fast-running red river. Just shy of losing consciousness, being brutally dragged up a set of steep, metal stairs, I felt every rung bruising my entire body. Hearing a door creak open, a cool breeze wafted across my face. Where am I? With blood pooled in my blackened eyes, I was shrouded in darkness. Suddenly, I was hoisted upright, and my last living memory was of being airborne. Yet, all I could think of was that *Superman Got Nothing On Me.*

About the Authors

Texas-born Baby Boomers, Jordan and Sharyn grew up in the idyllic 1950s. A rugged, entrepreneurial spirit shaped their values, work ethic, and resilience with a deep connection to the land.

As an East Lone Star State boy, he hailed from a family farm community surrounded by stunning Walnut, Pecan, and Red Oak hardwood forests.

As a West Texan gal, she grew up in an oil-rich area with expansive cotton farms and cattle ranches. Where Willow, Cherry, and Apricot trees lined the streets and populated the town square.

Coming of age during the 1960s with their front-row seat to the Vietnam War, Social Upheaval, and Civil Rights unrest wove a tapestry of freedom, justice, and peace. Now in their 70s, these beliefs still inform, inspire, and enrich their everyday love story.

Storyteller

Step into a world where courage and compassion lead the way and become a Storyteller, Bridge Builder, Storyteller, and Catalyst of Change, crafting a beautiful future for all. Stand against the corruption of evil politicians, champion truth and justice, bless others with beauty, joy, and peace, and inspire positive transformation. Discover

Witness the power of unity in the face of adversity and connectivity in a time of division and liberation in an era that attempts to suppress our freedoms. Let these adventures ignite a spark within you, encouraging gratitude, grace, and goodness to shine.

To receive a gift from Sharyn's Medicine Card Deck, the Angelic Realm of Synchronicity,

Email: windwaterwriterly@fengshuisimplified.com.

To continue Willow and Finn's timeless tales, go to fengshuisimplified.com

~Deep Bow

www.ingramcontent.com/pod-product-compliance
Lightning Source LLC
Chambersburg PA
CBHW051329020726
47501CB00007B/1985